Love's Persuasion

OLA AWONUBI

This edition is published in 2015 by Ankara Press

ISBN: 978-978-53151-4-1

One

Ada walked into the hotel where the end-of-year Christmas party was being held and looked around the plush foyer, decorated with fairy lights and a huge Christmas tree. The room was filled with her colleagues, some of whom complimented her on her outfit. Some women were wearing evening gowns or cocktail gowns whilst others had opted for traditional wear. The men were in suits or babban riga, dashikis or buba-and-sokotos.

The annual board meeting had been held earlier that day. There were changes brewing and everyone was apprehensive. There had been something in the air, etched on people's faces, chewed about in the canteen, discussed at their desks. The words 'restructure' and 'retrenchments' were whispered as people shrugged and looked into the sky, as if waiting for God to help them.

It must be serious, Ada thought.

Whatever was happening would be announced just before the party.

As people made small talk, Boney M's classic Christmas song 'Mary's Boy Child' filtered through the speakers discreetly tucked away in the corners of the room. It was immediately followed by Ebenezer Obey's 'Keresimesi Odun De'. The Christmas mood was really in the air.

Would it still linger after the night's announcements, Ada wondered.

She made her way to the ladies' room to check on her make-up and do her hair. She eyed herself critically in the mirror and applied some green-blue eye shadow and some lip gloss. She twisted her plaits into a chignon on the top of her head, which emphasised her long slender neck and high cheekbones. The look was completed by small gold earrings.

Ada was pleased with her reflection. Her outfit was simple and elegant: a blue and light-green number, its swirls of gold emphasised her slim waist. It skimmed her hips and fell to the ground in a train at the back. Initially, she had not wanted to go to the Christmas party and had said as much to her roommate Liz the week before. She needed to study for her upcoming tests in January and she really could not afford an evening gown. When she'd discovered that attendance at the party was mandatory, she'd opted for something already in her wardrobe. Though she'd been stressed about it, she had to admit that her look wasn't bad.

Dresses should be the last thing on her mind anyway. Who knew what would happen after tonight? The future was uncertain at City Finance and now the news was going to be broken to the staff before the party kicked off.

The door opened and Agatha swept in, jolting Ada's mind into reality. Agatha was wearing a short strapless purple dress and stole a glance at Ada, who was adjusting her outfit.

"Have you heard the news?" Agatha lowered her voice. "There is talk that M.D. is stepping down. There might be some restructuring.'

"Of course. It's on everyone's lips."

"You know Mr Obi – my brother's friend? He told me that he heard that Oga may be bringing in someone from abroad to take over from the M.D."

"I don't really listen to that man."

"Wetin dey do you sef? Mr Obi was just being friendly and you dey frown your face as if say you and the man be age mates."

"Agatha abeg leave me alone. I can't stand the man."

"Na you know jo." Her eyes narrowed as she took a good look at Ada. "Nice dress," she said. "Why are you fiddling with it?"

"I think it's a bit too low in front."

"Little Miss Innocenti. Don't tell me you never wear low-cut tops?" She stared at Ada. "What's that?"

Ada quickly tugged at her neckline. "What?"

"There's nothing wrong with my eyesight, you know. I can see clearly. That black mark on your chest?"

Ada shrugged and continued adjusting her dress. She had always been embarrassed by her birthmark. She wasn't vain but she'd grown up thinking that it was like throwing dark paint in the middle of an interesting landscape. She remembered how she used to hide in corners away from the prying eyes of other girls while changing for P.E. lessons.

"That looks like the kind of thing people bring with them from the spirit world."

"I don't believe in such nonsense."

"Remember the girl Ezinma in *Things Fall Apart*? She had a mark on her because she was an Ogbanje. Are you sure you're not a spirit child?"

Ada regretted entering into this conversation with the girl. It was ridiculous that Agatha was calling her an Ogbanje, a child who had died and yet kept taunting her parents by 'coming back' as a new-born. "I've got to go."

Agatha laughed. "You be Ogbanje, true, true! That's why una no wan answer the question!"

Ada, annoyed, hurried out of the ladies', leaving Agatha's laughter behind her. She smoothed down her outfit and, as her heel caught in the long skirt trailing behind her, she fell forward into the arms of a tall man emerging from the men's toilet. The man steadied her, a concerned look on his face.

"Sorry … I wasn't looking where I was going," he said. "Are you alright?"

Ada stared up at him for a moment, irritation from Agatha's taunts mingling with the embarrassment of falling into a stranger's arms. A good-looking stranger at that.

She frowned, trying to place the accent. It was foreign – English.

"I'm OK," she said, taking in his height and his finely tailored grey suit, which seemed to mould itself to his broad shoulders. Clean-shaven, cropped hair, with eyes a curious shade of light brown and, when he smiled, a dimple on his left cheek. Ada noticed his eyes taking in every iota of her appearance.

This bobo fine o, she concluded. *Maybe he is one of the guests in the hotel.*

His hands fell to his sides. "Are you sure?"

She nodded.

He smiled. "Well, goodnight then."

"Goodnight."

He moved past her and she continued on to rejoin her colleagues in the auditorium, which had been arranged theatre-style so that all the chairs were facing the main speaker. There was a tantalising aroma of hot savoury food that the stewards were putting out in the adjacent dining hall. She hadn't had a decent meal all day.

Ada took her seat and saw the man whom she had just bumped into in the corridor. He was setting up a projector at the front of the room and looking intently at a laptop. Surely such a well-dressed man could not be part of the hotel's IT crew?

Someone tapped her several times on her arm and she turned round in irritation. It was Olu.

Olu Smith, one of the accounts clerks, wasn't nicknamed Radio City Finance for nothing.

"Something dey happen o. I knew it. Guess what a little bird in M.D.'s office told me?"

Ada shrugged, knowing that he was going to tell her anyway.

"The new person coming to take over the company is Oga's son."

"The one that has been in England for all these years?"

Olu nodded.

"But what does he know about City Finance? And about the employees?"

"I think that's the golden boy from London …"

Olu nodded in the direction of the man on the podium, who was now looking through a set of papers in his hand.

"So, that's Oga's son?" Ada asked, surprised as she watched the board members enter. People started to scramble for their seats. She couldn't help noticing how proud the managing director looked when he walked up to talk to his son while the rest of the board took their seats at the front of the room.

"Oga's only beloved son. Summoned from London to take over his inheritance." Olu's voice was low and scathing. "Some people have all the luck, sha."

"Ssssh …" Ada whispered. "Let's hear what he has to say."

Two

"Good evening everyone." The man's voice was deep and confident. His English accent made him the object of everyone's attention. Pleasant yet firm, it had a note of authority and people immediately began to sit up and focus and the noise subsided.

"OK. I'm Tony Okoli and I am the new assistant managing director of City Finance. I have been asked by the managing director and the board of directors to increase our productivity and coordinate our overall resources. We need to start running a tighter operation. Our auditors are keen for us to put measures in place to increase our profit margin and maintain our market share. I look forward to meeting everyone individually in the coming weeks."

There were hums and murmurings from the crowd seated below him.

He switched on the projector and some graphs and flowcharts appeared. Ada watched him, impressed by his eloquence and confidence as he quoted figures and percentages.

"With introductions over, let's move on to what we need to do to keep us running smoothly. This is what we need to be making in order to cover our overheads – the gratuities that some of you are marking time to collect – and the salaries that – considering the amount of work that some of you do – may not all be entirely justified."

Ada's mouth fell open. *He is definitely straight to the point.*

"I have a question …" One of the department heads stood up, his arms folded across his chest.

Tony looked up and nodded. "Ah … Mr Coker, Human Resources. I thought you might have a question. Yes, how can I help you?"

Mr Coker looked taken aback that Okoli junior recognised him.

"With all due respect to the M.D. and the rest of the board, you just can't come here and start to insult us – we work hard here!"

"Yes, Mr Coker, I do realise this company owes a lot to the hard-working members of staff and, as a new member of the management team, I will make sure that such employees are rewarded for their diligence. However ..." his eyes fixed on the older man, "I will also do everything in my power to weed out the inefficient, the incompetent and the corrupt."

Mr Coker looked uncomfortable.

"Are you accusing anyone in particular?" Mr Coker stammered, wiping his brow.

"Our auditors are finalising their report and the management team will be in contact with the appropriate members of staff regarding certain discrepancies. I hope I have answered your question."

Tony Okoli picked up a batch of papers and continued,

waving them for emphasis. "These papers detail a few of the problems that are endemic in this organisation. Let me give you some examples: a staff member was being paid for an unsubstantiated three-year study leave, another for five years; salaries were being paid to deceased members of staff, and there are unapproved expenses for hotel bills, restaurant bills and even one manager's dry-cleaning bill."

Nervous laughter erupted from somewhere in the room. Tony shook his head.

"I'm glad someone finds it amusing. Our auditors don't. This cannot be allowed to continue if we want to keep this company viable. We must all work together to take ownership and get rid of the mentality of 'No be my papa's company.'"

Everyone laughed at the unexpected use of pidgin English. So, this wasn't some oyinbo boy – he had been 'cooked' enough in Nigeria to hold his own. His eyes swept around the room.

"We all have a duty to work hard to keep this company afloat and I want to encourage everyone to get on board and be part of the solution – and not the problem. If anyone wants to speak to me, or a member of the management team, about anything I have just said, please feel free to do so; we will be around. And, if you prefer to remain incognito, I will ask for a suggestions box to be put in the reception."

Ada felt another tap. Olu again.

"Inco …what …what does that mean?"

"Incognito, it means anonymous …," she whispered. *Who did he think she was – The Oxford Dictionary?*

Ada glared at him and turned back to the speaker, who was now rounding up.

"So, with the serious business out of the way … let's all head for the buffet, and have a good time."

There was applause when he turned off the projector and put his papers into a briefcase. She saw Chief Okoli and the other board members gather around him, their expressions serious.

Hmm … Something go happen o, Ada thought. *Heads will roll.*

No wonder so many of the top managers and heads of departments had been on edge lately. They had probably got wind that 'Mr War Against Indiscipline' was being brought in from London to come and sweep the company clean. The guy did have a point. She worked in accounts and often queried invoices and expenses, but she had been told by her manager that they had all been approved. A business could not operate a free-for-all philosophy – it had to have boundaries, structure and control. She knew that from her business and finance course.

People moved off to the dining area in groups, discussing the speech, and as Ada mingled with her colleagues, she saw Agatha approaching. She turned away from her, still irritated by their last exchange.

Agatha appeared next to her and joined in the chatter.

"The man fine, sha … I wonder if he is single."

The other colleague laughed. "Haba – the man tell you say he dey look for wife?"

"All single men need a wife. They just don't know it."

Ada gave her a dirty look. It was clear the girl had not been listening to a word Tony Okoli had said. She was more occupied with his looks and how good he looked in his suit.

Dismissing Agatha from her mind, Ada walked off to get herself a glass of bitter lemon at the bar, and passed Tony Okoli in discussion with Mrs Oseni, the head of accounts and her manager. She nodded a greeting to both and began to move on, but Mrs Oseni called her back.

"Speaking of conscientious employees … I would like to introduce you to Ada Okafor."

Tony looked at her intently, their eyes meeting and they shook hands.

Mrs Oseni was full of praise. "I don't know how she does it. She works on reception, helps out in accounts twice a week to get experience and is doing a part-time business and finance course."

Tony's eyes flickered with interest. "Hello, Ada. Sounds like you are exactly the kind of employee we need." His handshake was firm as he smiled at her.

"Thank you." Ada took a good look at him. He had eyes that seemed to see straight through you. It was clear that he had inherited his good looks from his mother, whom Ada saw occasionally when she came into the office.

Where his father was dark, stocky and quiet, Tony Okoli was trim and spritely. He had his mother's winning smile.

Mrs Oseni moved off, leaving Tony and Ada to talk.

"So, where are you studying?"

"Unilag."

They walked around the room for a while, talking. He told her that his sister had spent her first year at the University of Lagos before she had gone abroad.

They joined the queue for the buffet.

When she reached the table, Ada picked up a plate. She looked at the spread of food and wondered whether to help herself to some of the delicious-looking jollof rice or the curried chicken and salad.

"I think I'll try some of the rice. It looks fantastic."

Tony was standing next to her, plate in hand, smiling.

Boy, this guy was fine. Like Majid Michel – just a shade darker in complexion.

She felt his eyes sweeping over her. Her body flushed hot and cold and her heart beat faster. She could not seem to tear her gaze away from his. At that moment a short, squat figure pushed past her and addressed the new assistant managing director.

"Mr Ignatius Obi," he said, introducing himself to Tony. "I am the accounts manager for the whole southwest region."

A dark-skinned man, with small bulbous eyes, he was of average height and in his early fifties. Her eyes rested on his swollen belly, a testament to years of indulging in too much Guinness and pepper soup. He had roving eyes and she intensely disliked his habit of sexually harassing junior members of staff.

Ada saw Tony Okoli's eyes narrow - not too pleased at the intrusion either - but he adopted a polished smile that didn't quite reach his eyes as he shook Mr Obi's hand.

Then Mr Obi began piling his plate with food as if he was afraid it would grow legs and run away. She saw Tony's eyes widen in amazement as the mountain of food on the plate grew steadily.

"Really? That's a pretty impressive title."

"My responsibilities are many, sir. That's what I want to talk to you about – you said anyone who has suggestions about how we can maximise profit should talk to you." He bent down and shovelled another piece of beef onto his plate. Ada thought she could hear the plate groan.

"Are you sure you have enough there?" Tony asked. But his irony was lost on the older man. Ada smiled and Tony caught her eyes. As they exchanged a look, a small smile flitted across his face. Then she suddenly saw Tony's serious side as he turned to the older man.

"We can have a chat after I have finished eating. Alternatively, you can put your suggestions in the box and the management team will go through them and discuss those that are workable."

"OK, sir," Mr Obi said with a bow. Ada marvelled at how well Tony was dealing with the man. She wished she could get rid of him that easily.

Mr Obi was about to add another bow, when he

spotted Ada standing to the side, quietly observing the interaction. He straightened up, puffed out his chest like a cockerel and looked at her with pointed lechery.

"You are looking very beautiful, Ada," he said, practically salivating.

Ada's lips tightened. The guy made her skin crawl.

"I will come back as soon as I've finished eating ... maybe we could have a dance?" he laughed.

"I don't think so."

Mr Obi laughed again and went off with his food. Ada watched him go, her eyes narrowed.

"I take it that Mr Obi is not someone whose opinion you value," Tony Okoli said.

"You are very observant."

"Ah. Tact and diplomacy. Very good qualities." Tony smiled again. "Can I get you a drink?"

"Coke please," as they walked towards the bar.

"So, what do *you* think this company needs to maximise sales, to make it a leader in this competitive market?" He handed her a glass.

"Research and development, training for middle-level management, targeted marketing and new markets," she said promptly.

He gave her a look, clearly impressed.

"You have definitely given me food for thought. I would really appreciate it if you would drop a line in the suggestions box."

"Of course." *Does he think that all clerks were happy*

to sit pounding away at a computer all their lives? Her lips curved into a small smile.

Tony smiled. "So, how long have you been working here?"

"Two years."

"Do you like it?"

"Yes. It's a great place to work and there are lots of opportunities to advance, and the managers ... well, most of them have principles and morals."

"That's good. I'm glad you think so ... and you're not just saying that because you're talking to me."

She looked at him. "I don't say what I don't mean."

"Another admirable quality. It's good to see that City Finance has such dedicated staff members."

Ada found herself at a loss for words, which was very unlike her.

A slow ballad was playing. She looked up and caught his eyes and they both smiled at the same time.

"John Legend." As he bent to hear her, she felt the warmth of his breath fanning her neck and a shiver cascade down her spine.

"Do you like him?"

She nodded. "'Ordinary People' is my favourite."

"Me too."

He looked down at her and she saw a hint of hesitation in his eyes. Then he bent closer to hers.

"Ada, despite what you said about ..."

"Yes?"

He was about to say something when one of the directors came up to him and whispered in his ear. He nodded and turned to Ada. "I need to speak to one of our board members. Thank you for your insights, Ada. It's been very nice talking to you."

"You're welcome," she smiled as he left.

***

Tony Okoli was having a conversation with a prospective client to whom his father had introduced to him. Yet, he was only half-listening. He was wondering why he hadn't asked the beautiful Miss Okafor for a dance earlier. His eyes floated over the sea of faces and he saw her leaving the room. His memories were of smooth chocolate skin, long legs, a tiny waist, curves that could play havoc with any man's mind – and a razor-sharp business mind.

Ada Okafor. Not a name to be forgotten. Not a figure to be forgotten, either. He smiled to himself.

It was good to be back in Nigeria.

Three

Just before midnight, Ada got a lift back to the house where she shared a room with Liz.

There was a medium-sized sofa bed and wardrobe that they shared, two chairs, a small wooden table and their tiny colour TV – their one extravagance bought at a sale at Mile 12 market. All the furniture was slightly worn and the room a bit cramped. They shared the bathroom and kitchen with the rest of the tenants. On a good day the house would be filled with the aroma of fried chicken or puff puff from the landlady's shop in front of the house. Other days it would be the strong smells coming from the bathroom or the outside toilet struggling for domination.

Liz looked up from the Nollywood drama she was watching on TV.

"Una don come? How was it?"

Ada shrugged. "Nice party. Good food. Great music."

"You look fantastic … so, did you manage to find a prince, or did a prince find you?"

"Na you know o, Liz." Ada kicked off her high-heeled strappy sandals and sank into the sofa. "No be Prince I go find there."

"So, you want to tell me that nobody complimented you sha?"

"There were a few." She remembered the admiring look Tony Okoli had given her when they had been introduced, followed by the conversation they had. He seemed genuinely interested in listening to what she had to say. Then she recalled how Mr Obi's bulbous eyes seemed to bore into her while he was looking her up and down, but she pushed that memory to the back of her mind.

"I did get to speak to a really nice guy," Ada said.

Liz had a mischievous smile on her face.

"So, tell me more."

"He spoke well, had lovely manners and a really nice smile. When he smiles – his cheeks goes in like this." She stuck a finger into her cheek, imitating Tony's dimple. "It is kind of cute."

"Na 'cute' we go chop? Abeg, does this man have money?"

Ada smiled. "Liz una don come o."

"Did he get your number?"

Ada shook herself out of her dreams. "No."

"Ah-ah, you met this wonderful man and you didn't give him your number?"

"Liz, he was busy … we only spoke for a few minutes."

"So, who is this mystery man sef? One of your colleagues?"

"His name is Tony. There was a point when I almost thought he was going to ask me to dance with him."

"Really?"

"Really."

"What of that toad Mr Obi?" Liz asked.

"When did toad become man?" Ada shot back, hissing.

They both burst out laughing.

"So, this Tony, the guy seems really cool."

"Don't go there. He is the new assistant managing director – na Oga's son. He's the second-in-command to Oga pata pata – and, besides, these people like to date rich people like themselves. You know, keep the money in the family."

"But you said he was about to ask you to dance with him?"

Ada shrugged. "Maybe, maybe not." Maybe she'd imagined it. Maybe her mind had been playing tricks on her. He was charming and had listened to all she had to say, but that didn't mean he was attracted to her. She had to admit, it had been nice to talk to a really good-looking man with manners – it wasn't every day she met such people – but she needed to get back to reality. It was time to fold up her outfit and pack it away, and with it, all these silly thoughts.

***

When Ada arrived at the office first thing on Monday morning, she headed for reception and took her seat. Nike, one of her colleagues from accounts, was talking to Agatha.

Ada had woken up with a headache, a result of staying up most of the night before trying to study her resource management module. She was not in the mood for chit-chat. "See who?"

"What did you think of the new Oga? He looked a bit like Majid Michel. Just darker," said Agatha, who was staring into space. "I saw him this morning when the M.D. was showing him around. He smiled at me."

"Really?"

Nike shook her head. "The bobo is handsome sha. I saw him near the buffet afterwards but he was deep in conversation with the other directors, and there were so many people wanting to talk to him that I gave up in the end. The food was nice, but talking to him would have been nicer."

"The man sound like oyinbo. You no hear am?" Agatha sighed.

Ada picked up her headphones and pressed the flashing green button for the next caller. It was a good that her interaction with the object of their fantasies had gone unnoticed. Gossip was the last thing she needed. Unlike Agatha, she wasn't in awe of the rich and famous.

"I wish I could meet someone like that. We would get married and travel the world together," Agatha said sighing.

Ada transferred the call and looked at her colleague. "Agatha, you've been watching too many romantic comedies."

"He is such a gentleman. He opened the door for me this morning, you know," Agatha continued, ignoring Ada's comment. "Imagine a Naija man opening a door for me … London is good o."

Ada stopped listening and pulled out a file. That was Agatha for you. She was always falling for some fine bobo, and it always got her into trouble.

But he is fine. Na fine I go chop? she asked herself.

She was so tired of listening to the way some of her women friends kept going on about men – it was like they were waiting for a man to come along before they started living. Yet, as soon as they got married, their mother-in-law would start demanding grandchildren, and, the minute those arrived, that was the end of their careers. The degree they had spent years studying for would be framed and stuck on the sitting room wall, like a portrait in a museum. The husband of such a woman would pound his chest in pride.

"See my wife, she has a BA, MA and PhD and yet she is content to be a housewife and look after all these children I have given her!" Such men would humour their wives with occasional trips abroad and might even open a shop for them. People would bow and call her 'Madam'. Nobody would care that she was entirely reliant on her husband for everything, that she did not possess one kobo of her own.

No, she had sworn that would never happen to her. She wasn't going to end up like some of her friends, relying on their rich boyfriends or sugar daddies to survive. That was why she was working so hard, to make sure that she could take care of herself. In her previous job, her manager had only been interested in one thing, and her refusal to give it to him had stood in her way of being promoted. But while she might not have a fantastic flat, the latest car or expensive clothes to wear, she had her self-respect.

She had been delighted to land a job at City Finance, a much bigger firm. It was a joy to realise that everyone got on with their job and there was none of that nonsense of managers using their positions to bully junior members of staff. Except Mr Obi, with his persistent unwanted advances. Every time the man opened his mouth she was reminded of the open gutter in front of her house. She resolved to continue to ignore him; he was not her boss and, except when he came to chase invoices and cheques for suppliers, she had very little to do with him. She peered at the computer screen and banged away at the keyboard, imagining she was banging at Mr Obi's head.

***

The weeks after the staff Christmas party were a whirlwind of work and studies. That meant sometimes she had to work late in order to get her work done and, with her boss's permission, use the computer to type out her assignments.

On one of those evenings she had stayed behind to finish off a report.

"Hey, beautiful." She looked up and saw Mr Obi standing in the doorway. She took a deep breath.

"What are you doing here so late?" she asked irritably.

"Important work, important work. People don't understand the importance of getting a job done properly. You see my point?"

"Mr Obi, I have never seen your point," she said, giving him a withering glance and continuing with her work.

He slinked up to her desk and stood over her, leering.

"Imagine this. Me and you, in the office, at night all alone."

"We are not alone," she said, eyeing him. "There are still other people here."

"But they are on the floor below us. This floor is empty. I know because I saw them leave one by one."

She stopped typing. "Mr Obi, please leave me alone and go away before I call security."

"Don't be like that. I was just trying to be friendly."

She resumed her typing and said nothing, hoping he would take the hint, but he just stood there, rubbing his chin.

"Ada, why are you frowing, eh?" he asked finally. "Is it a crime for a man to like a woman?"

"You no dey shame. I am an employee here and you are a married man."

He laughed at that. "That's what I like about you. You are not the kind of girl that makes things easy for a man. You want me to really chase you and shower you with gifts. I know you girls – suppose I get you a nice gold necklace?"

She ignored him and kept on working. He cocked his head to one side as if trying to puzzle her out.

"You just want to suffer, eh? I heard you are trying to pay for your university course. I can pay that, one time. Put you up in a nice flat. Get you a little car?"

Ada stopped typing. "Please try and respect yourself, Mr Obi. You are old enough to be my dad. Let this be the first and the last of this kind of harassment – if not, I will have to report it to management."

He shook his head and laughed and laughed, doubling over.

"Every woman has her price," he said when he'd finally stopped laughing. He leaned over the desk and touched her face; she jerked away, swatting his hand. "Give me time. When I discover yours, I will get you ..." he snapped his fingers, "just like that."

Ada smelled the alcohol and the stench of stale cigarettes that clung to the man like a second skin and her stomach tightened in nausea. The realisation dawned on her that she was alone in the office with a lecherous man who had been drinking. He had motive and now he had opportunity. She felt her heartbeat accelerate.

She was amazed at her how firm her voice sounded. "In your dreams."

"Eh? Dreams can come true, you know. Don't make me go and see a jujuman to get you o."

He was threatening her with juju? She was incredulous. It was a good job she didn't believe in all that, but maybe it was time to talk to somebody in human resources?

He laughed again and left the room a bit unsteadily. Only when he shut the door behind him did she feel her heartbeat begin to return to normal.

Then, the door opened again and all her irritation and anger erupted.

"Just go away and leave me alone!" she shouted.

"Ada?"

It was Tony Okoli, his eyebrows raised, bemused at her outburst. He closed the door behind him and leaned against it.

"What was all that about?"

"I – I thought you were someone else," she said, suddenly embarrassed. *What did he see? What did he hear?* she wondered frantically.

He looked at her. "There is hardly anyone about."

Mr Obi must have been quicker on his feet than she gave him credit for. She tried to focus on the screen in front of her. "I'm sorry for shouting."

"I understand. Colleagues can have that effect," he joked. "I know that feeling too well ..."

Ada found herself relaxing and managed a smile. "I guess it's just been a long day."

He looked at his watch. "Do you usually work this late?"

"Sometimes."

"Why's that?"

"I leave work early on Tuesdays and Wednesdays to make my classes at the university. So, sometimes I need to stay late to finish my work."

"Yes, I remember you told me you were studying

part-time at Unilag. Business and finance, wasn't it?"

"Yes." Ada was surprised that he had remembered their conversation. He must have spoken to hundreds of people at the party.

"That's one of the things I would like to change around here – get more people studying part-time so they can improve themselves professionally. I know there are a few in H.R. studying for their Chartered Institute of Personnel Management exam."

"That would be really good."

"I'm glad you think so." He smiled again, looking down at her and Ada felt a bit self-conscious. Then she realised that he was actually looking at something on her desk.

"You have great taste," he said. She followed his gaze to her copy of *Half of a Yellow Sun* by Chimamanda Ngozi Adichie.

"You started reading it yet?" he asked, picking up the book.

"I've read it twice," Ada said. "I think it's brilliant, but then some might say we are biased. It is our story, after all. I just love her attention to historical detail, the way she uses words, the characters and their stories. It reminds me of all the stuff my parents told me about the Biafran War."

He looked at her. "My parents hardly talk about it."

"It has always been controversial," she said, shrugging thoughtfully. "People see it in so many different ways –

for some, it is just a part of history and we are supposed to move on from it."

Tony laughed. It was short and sharp and had a regretful tinge to it. "I went searching for my history. It didn't come looking for me."

Ada wanted to ask more questions, but realised that he was looking at his watch.

"Look at me, nattering on about books. I've made you stay even later than you were planning to ..."

"It's OK, I love books. I will even spend money I don't have to buy a book."

"Ada, every time I meet you, it's always a pleasure. Maybe ..." he hesitated and then continued a little more casually, "... we can discuss the books we love over a coffee or a drink – one day."

Ada nodded before she even realised what she had done. Smiling broadly, he turned and walked towards the door.

"Goodnight, Ada."

"Goodnight, Mr Okoli."

"Don't stay too late."

"Er ... I won't."

Her mouth was still open when the door closed behind him.

***

Tony Okoli walked down the corridor away from Ada's office, searching for the keys of his car. He shook his head, feeling foolish and trying to get the conversation he'd just had out of his mind.

What was all that about? "Maybe we can discuss our love of books over a coffee one day?" Okoli, surely you could have been more original than that, for goodness' sake?

What on earth was he doing – fantasising about some girl at work whom he had just met? OK, so she was a stunner. So, her eyes were deep, dark pools that a man could dive into and her lips were so firm that it seemed they were just begging to be kissed and her … *OK, Okoli, that's enough!* he admonished himself before his mind could move on to her other physical attributes. He was engaged to Gloria. This daydreaming about Ada was absolutely crazy.

The girl was attractive, no doubt, but he just liked the fact that she was ambitious, loved books, spoke her mind, was hard-working, and didn't seem intimidated by his position: that's all.

Honestly, that's all it is.

Four

Mrs Okoli glowed with contentment as she observed her family around the table. Her two children – Tony and his younger sister, Samantha – were both in the country and she was enjoying it while it lasted. Jollof rice, chicken and plantain, followed by fruit salad and ice cream was served.

Chief Okoli said very little to his son, but focused more on his daughter.

His wife noticed and tried to lighten the atmosphere between the two men she loved.

"We are so happy that you are back, Tony."

Chief Okoli muttered. "Finally."

Tony was about to respond, then decided against it and carried on eating his meal.

Samantha poured herself some fruit juice. "Dad, I was thinking about working alongside Tony. I would love the chance to get on board and start using everything from my business degree."

Her father snorted. "That won't take us very far, will it? Most of what they teach in these business schools has nothing to do with the real world of business."

Mrs Okoli looked at her daughter and then at her husband.

"Don't mind your dad. He is always talking about how proud he is of you both."

Samantha's face hardened, she attacked the food on her plate.

Silence filled the room.

Then Samantha spoke again. "What on earth do you want me to do – just stay at home and watch TV?"

Her father laughed but it was devoid of amusement. "If you got some pointers from your mother on how to keep a good home I don't think it would be a bad thing. That boy you are dating is planning on marrying you one day, you know."

"There is more to life than marriage, dad. Maybe I want more from life than what mum does."

"When you are a quarter of a fingernail of the woman your mother is – then you can begin to make such statements."

Samantha stood up, pushed her chair back and ran upstairs. Her mother shook her head and followed her, leaving the two men together.

"Dad—"

"I have spent my life building up my businesses for you, and all you want to do is stay in London doing this writing thing you say is so important to you. I've let you do your own thing, but now it's time for you to take over the reins and shoulder your responsibility. You are 28 now – almost 30. Do you think I sent you to the University of London to become the next Chinua Achebe? You have a degree in business and finance and your ACCA for a reason, you know."

Tony's face tightened. "I know my responsibilities. That's why I came back."

His father seemed to relax. "And all this stuff about writing – this hobby of yours. Finally got that out of your system?"

Tony opened his mouth and was about to reply when his mother came back into the room with a petulant Samantha.

His mother sat down, a determined look on her face. "Now we are going to have a quiet, civilised dinner. No talk about the business."

Chief Okoli helped himself to more food. Tony swallowed the speech he had prepared for his father along with a glass of water.

Now is not the time.

Mrs Okoli turned to her son. "So, have you heard from Gloria?"

Tony nodded. "Yeah. Yeah. She's fine and sends her love. I love this jollof rice, Mum. Just as I like it."

His mother smiled.

Later on, Tony sat on the veranda talking to Samantha, who was in an uncharacteristically reflective mood.

"It's great having you back."

He shrugged. "Dad needed help."

"What about your writing? That's why you left the job in the city to go work in that publishing house. To pursue your writing."

"It was the happiest moment in my life. It didn't pay

much but it was one of the most fulfilling things I have ever done. Then I found out about Dad ... blood pressure, stress ... you know the rest."

Samantha sighed. "I told them I could help out. I studied for this – for goodness' sake. Why won't he give me a chance?"

"I said exactly the same thing ... but he just thought I was trying to shirk my responsibilities."

They both fell silent.

"Mum's up there now, trying to get him to calm down, take his medication and get off the phone and forget about work."

"I don't fancy her chances. Dad is ..."

They both laughed. "Dad."

Samantha smiled. "So, what's it like being back?"

Tony shrugged.

***

Two weeks later, Ada was working at reception with Agatha. The entrance foyer was a large space, with cream walls, plush furniture and a reception point situated in the middle. Some of the managers were standing on one side talking in hushed tones when Tony Okoli came in and walked up to the reception desk.

He looked a bit different; his dimple was not in evidence today and his manner was businesslike. He greeted both of them.

"Good morning, ladies."

"Good morning, Mr Okoli," Ada answered politely. Agatha seemed to be at a loss for words. She sat staring at the man's moving mouth.

"I'm having an important meeting in the Europa Suite on the fourth floor. Please show any visitors up when they come in," he said briskly. "It starts at 9.30am – and I mean 9.30 sharp. If anyone arrives late, tell them not to bother."

"But …" Agatha had finally found her voice, but he had already headed off towards the lifts.

Ada turned back to the computer and continued working on her accounts spreadsheet.

"See me see trouble o," Agatha whispered desperately, turning to Ada. "How can I tell the heads of H.R. and strategy that they can't attend the meeting if they come late? The two of them are professional latecomers. Especially that Mr Coker."

Ada nodded in agreement, but said nothing. In her head, she tried to reconcile the man she had spoken to about books a few weeks earlier with the one who seemed so distant and cold just now. *Maybe he was just being professional*, she thought.

The visitors arrived, signed the register and were given visitors' badges. Agatha took them up in the lift to the meeting room and returned to reception.

A few minutes later Ada and Agatha watched Mr Coker rushing in, clearly desperate to be on time.

"Oga don come?"

Agatha nodded. "Yes sir."

Mr Coker hurried to the lifts as fast as he could.

The women exchanged looks and laughed.

"Fear of embarrassment is a good motivator o." Ada smiled.

"Na true o."

"Amazing! Agatha exclaimed. "Do you know that when I took that oyinbo up to the meeting room, most of the usual latecomers were already in the room? I think they realise that this small boy can embarrass them if they don't comply with his directions."

"Trouble dey come o." Agatha whispered.

Ada looked up and saw a dark-skinned young woman walking towards reception. She was petite and curvy and wore a pink and black Chanel-style jacket over a tight black skirt that ended just above the knees. Her high black patent shoes tapped against the polished marble as she marched towards them. Her hair had been cut into a short Rihanna weave and her lips, which glistened with clear gloss, were fixed into a pout. She plonked her Chanel bag down on the reception desk.

Ada sighed to herself. Tony's younger sister, Samantha, was a general pain in the neck.

"Is Tony in?" the young woman demanded in a high-pitched whiny voice with a hint of an American accent.

"He is in a meeting at the moment," Agatha replied.

"I need to see him." The young woman flashed a look at her.

"It's a very important meeting. He has asked not to be disturbed," said Ada.

The younger woman stared at Ada in barely concealed contempt. Ada squared her shoulders and met the younger woman's eyes coolly. "Do you know who I am?"

"Yes, Miss Okoli, I am quite aware of who you are, but Mr Okoli has left clear instructions not to be disturbed while he is in the meeting."

Ada ignored Agatha's gasp, and continued in a calm and even tone. "Would you like to take a seat and wait for him?"

Samantha gave her a look that could have killed and, without any warning, hurried towards the lifts. Ada wasn't prepared for this.

"Miss Okoli!" Ada called out as she got up and ran towards the lift but Samantha was too fast for her and Ada was just in time to see the smirk on her face as the lift doors closed.

Behind her, Agatha was laughing.

"You were a big help," Ada said irritably. "Thanks, eh. One day she will do the same to you and I will see how you handle it." She pressed the button for the second lift and waited for it to come down.

"You could always say that you had to go to the toilet and I was on the phone and she slipped past me," Agatha said, still laughing.

The second lift came down; Ada got into it and pressed the button for the fourth floor. She watched the displa lighting up with each floor it passed.

Tony Okoli had been polite to her the other night, but this was him in his official capacity – who knew what he might do to exert his authority? She couldn't afford to lose this job. Her lips tightened. She was not going to allow anyone to get her into trouble for trying to do what she was asked to do.

The lift stopped and she got out. This was the executive floor where all the meeting rooms and the offices of the directors, including Tony's, were situated. The décor was traditional with wood-panelled doors and plush carpeting. Unlike the rest of the building, it was quiet and restrained. She rushed past some senior members of staff and headed to the Europa meeting room at the end of the hallway.

Just as she reached the meeting room, Samantha burst out of it, banging the door shut behind her, and glared at Ada. Then Samantha stomped past her and made her way back to the lifts, without saying a word. Ada looked at the meeting room door with raised eyebrows.

This Tony Okoli is no pushover, she thought. *Not even with his own family.*

By the time Ada got back to reception, Samantha had left.

Five

One evening two weeks later Ada left the office and was swallowed up by the crowd of office workers, market women and traders. The roar of traffic competed with the newspaper vendor tooting his horn announcing to the world that the *PM News* was half-price for that day only. She passed a woman frying puff puff, the sweet aroma tantalising her nostrils as she made her way to Idumota bus stop. She sighed when she saw the sea of passengers waiting for transport home.

She caught a glimpse of herself in a shop window. Her hair was freshly plaited and tied back in neat ponytail, and she was wearing the bright-green blouse Liz had bought her for her birthday, along with the black skirt she liked because she thought it highlighted her legs. She'd finished the outfit with a huge black belt that made her waist look impossibly small.

Then a gold Nissan Pathfinder drew up next to the bus stop and someone called her name. The driver wound down the window and, with a shock, she saw it was Tony Okoli. Looking around, she noticed the looks on the faces of her fellow commuters and was immediately embarrassed. They probably thought he was trying to pick her up. *Fine girl, rich guy with a nice car; who could resist?* they all seemed to say.

"Hello!" he called to her. Tony had taken off his

sunglasses and was peering at her, as if he wanted to be sure he hadn't made a mistake.

Ada wished she could blend into the crowd. She waved hesitantly, but made no move to approach the car.

"Where are you going?" Tony shouted.

"Surulere," Ada replied. She could see the other commuters exchanging looks.

"Can I give you a lift?" he asked

"I'm fine," she said, shaking her head. "Don't worry."

"Na wa for you," said a middle-aged woman who was fanning herself next to her. "Someone is offering you a ride home and you dey make shakara. Una wan roast here?"

"Maybe the man is her boyfriend … una don fight, abi wetin?" a young wit added.

She could see a traffic policeman in his yellow shirt and red trousers walking menacingly towards them. It dawned on Ada that she was attracting more attention by staying at the bus stop than accepting his offer, so she gave in and walked towards the car.

As soon as she got in he drove away, the tyres screeching.

"I wouldn't want to take you out of your way," she said reaching for the seat belt.

"I don't mind, really."

As he roared off, she noted he was acclimatising to his country and its ways. If you were going to drive in Lagos, you had better look *sharp*.

"So, how are you?" he asked. She caught his quick glance as his eyes swept over her.

"I'm fine."

They found themselves in a go-slow as they reached Carter Bridge and Tony turned the engine off. He punched her address into his car's satnav. They watched the army of informal traders selling CDs, magazines, soft drinks and snacks darting in and out of the traffic.

"So, read any more good books lately?" Tony asked.

"I discovered a copy of *Great Expectations* yesterday at work. I can't remember how long it's been there, but I had a strong desire to read it again."

"Dickens, I love his work."

"I like Estella."

"Really? Why?"

"She is a strong woman. She makes her own decisions and refuses to let society mould her into a victim, unlike her mentor, Miss Havisham."

"She is also cruel and vindictive. Just like Miss Havisham. Not a good role model at all I'd say."

"So, what's your favourite Dickens novel?"

"*A Tale of Two Cities*. It sums up everything that is noble about man, love, friendship and loyalty, leading to the ultimate sacrifice and Sydney Carton's immortal words: 'It is a far, far better thing that I do, than I have ever done'… care to finish for me? Go on, I know you want to."

He gave her an encouraging look, and she couldn't help but smile as she finished the quote.

"'It is a far, far better rest that I go to than I have ever known.' I remember cramming huge chunks of the book for my literature exam when I was in Form Four."

He laughed at that. "You sound as if literature means a lot to you. How did you end up in the world of high finance?"

"I could ask you the same question."

"That's a long story and it will probably take more time than we have on this bridge to tell it," he said soberly. Brightening, he added, "Besides, it involves my family and it's very tedious. A bit like a very bad fiction."

"Or like Nollywood?" she said, giggling.

"Sometimes. So, tell me about you. You haven't answered my question: what made you decide to go into finance?"

She told him about her studies at the university and her intention to obtain an MBA one day.

Tony looked across at her. "I spent my early childhood in Lagos and then I was sent to boarding school in England when I was ten, only coming home for the holidays."

"So, what did you study at university?" she asked.

"Accountancy for first degree, and then I did the final exams of the ACCA, Association of Chartered Certified Accountants," he offered.

"Impressive! Your parents must be proud."

"With my father's health scare, he asked me to come back and manage the head office," he said.

"What about your sister, Samantha? Doesn't she get

a say in how the business is run – if it's a family-run thing?"

"My sister … well, as my father says, 'She's just a girl. She will get married and go to her husband's house and let her degree become redundant.'"

"Really?"

"The English have family; they just don't remain bound to the cords of family expectation out of obligation and duty. Sometimes, in Nigeria we have to know how to balance things out – where to draw the line. Some of our customs are wonderful and others …" Tony sighed. "There are times when I find it all a bit too much." She wondered what he meant but did not want to pry. Instead she kept quiet and stared out of the window. They were now inching their way down to Ijora.

He sighed and continued, as if talking to himself: "My father has a lot of old-fashioned ideas about women, ones I don't agree with. I think Sam is tired of cooling her feet at home. She would rather be working alongside me … Anyway, I wanted to thank you for the professional way you handled her attempt to gate-crash my meeting a few weeks ago."

Ada shrugged. "I was just doing my job."

"You've got guts," he said, laughing. "I know she gave you a hard time. Sam likes to get her own way. I made it very clear that I wasn't impressed at being interrupted in the middle of important negotiations with clients. Honestly, the girl thinks the whole world revolves around her."

"It's OK. I can handle myself."

"I know, and now Sam knows too," he chuckled to himself. He glanced at her. "Anyway – I can see you like your job and that says a lot. Satisfied employees always go the extra mile."

She briefly considered telling him about her encounters with Mr Obi, but decided against it. She really did not want to take the man's irritating behaviour up with management. She couldn't be sure how Mr Obi would twist the situation if she reported it and she didn't see any reason to take a heavy-handed approach to something that was under control. Besides, she couldn't afford to lose this job. The managers were competent, workers were judged by their merit and there were opportunities for training and advancement. *He wouldn't understand what it's like to struggle*, she thought. He had probably had everything handed to him on a plate.

"Yes, I like it at City Finance."

"Well, I'm glad you like it. We must be doing something right."

"It's a great place."

He looked at her and smiled. "You are a great employee."

She was taken aback by his compliment. "Oh ... thanks."

Ada looked out of the window, at a loss for words. Warmth spread up from her stomach. It was almost suffocating.

What is wrong with you? she thought to herself. *This isn't the first good-looking man you have met, so why are you behaving like some dizzy schoolgirl?* She hardly knew him, yet he had the ability to affect her like this. She had to hold it together.

I know your type, Tony Okoli, and I'm not going to allow myself to be sidetracked by any 'fine boy'.

Then the traffic started moving again and he turned the key in the ignition.

"So, what's on the horizon for you? Career or marriage?"

She was conscious that he was steering the conversation in a different direction.

"Are they mutually exclusive? I see no reason why I can't be a happily married top-level financial analyst."

"But we both know that those often don't go hand in hand."

She was irritated by this, as if he felt what she wanted out of life was an unattainable dream. "I see no reason why my husband and I cannot be involved in managing our household together. It is impossible to expect a woman to hold down a full-time job, look after children and cook and clean all by herself. Any man who expects a woman to double as cook, lover, and dutiful daughter-in-law to all his relatives might as well go marry a robot."

"Well, I—"

But she didn't let him finish. "Our society is very patriarchal. 'You can read all the books from A to Z' as

43

my mother used to say, and still be regarded as a sexual object or baby-making machine. When I get married I will have to be on equal footing with my husband. I will be his partner, not his sidekick like the Lone Ranger and Tonto!"

When Tony didn't respond, Ada felt thoroughly embarrassed about her outburst.

Then he glanced at her and grinned mischievously.

"Whoooah … I was only kidding. I didn't mean to get your back up. Actually, I agree with you. Women need to be recognised for the work they do. I mean, my mother used to work when we were younger and my father was all for it. It was great seeing you on your soapbox again, though. And the Lone Ranger and Tonto bit was just priceless!"

Ada wanted to say something more but her thoughts were interrupted by the crisp voice on the satnav.

"*You have reached your destination.*"

They drew up in front of her house. Ada felt embarrassed about where she lived. The brown paint was peeling off the exterior, making it look like a wrinkly old cocoyam. Half-clothed children played on the veranda and a group of young men were playing pool in front of the house. Their landlady sat in the little kiosk outside frying yam. She looked up when she saw the expensive car.

Compared to his big mansion in Ikoyi, this probably looks like a slum, she thought. If she was honest with herself, it *was* a slum, but it was home – for now.

"I really enjoyed our conversation, Ada."

"I enjoyed it too," she replied. And she meant it. She hadn't had as much fun chatting with a member of the opposite sex in a long time. "Thanks for the lift."

The car stopped and she put her hand on the door handle. It didn't open. She tugged at the handle a few more times. Tony reached across her and he tried to open the door. At that split second her eyes caught his.

"What's wrong with the door?" she asked, trying to calm herself, wondering why her heart was beating so fast. His face so close to hers that she felt as if she was drowning in his expensive cologne.

He leaned forward and let his hand gently brush against her face.

"Ada …"

She blinked at him. All she could hear was her heart. He was staring down at her, a brooding look on his face as if he was lost in thought.

Then to her relief the door opened. She was free. He mumbled something about her taking care of herself and she clambered out as fast as she could, trying to compose herself.

She was confused.

What happened back there? This guy has the ability to turn my emotions into jelly. For a second I could have sworn he was about to kiss me. That look in his eyes … as he leaned over me.

She tried to compose herself. "Thanks for the lift."

Then he smiled. Too much, in her opinion. "No problem. Have a good evening, Ada."

"You too," she murmured and practically sprinted inside.

***

He waited until she had closed the door behind her before he pressed a button to lock the doors. A small smile played around his lips.

Okoli, you ought to be ashamed of yourself.

He shook his head, sighed, then drove off.

Later that evening, Tony stood on the balcony of his two-bedroomed house, soaking in the Ikoyi view. He could see little lights like fireflies dotting the darkness around him, coming from the homes of the ambassadors and consuls nearby. He turned his attention to the sheaf of documents in his hand and went through the contents again. He was taking work home regularly now. He sighed. It had to be done; people's jobs depended on it. The company was losing too much money and was beginning to be overtaken by its competitors.

City Finance was overloaded at the top management level. It reminded him of a tall house with a top floor so heavy that it threatened the structure of the whole building. It needed more mid-level management staff and less of the deadwood that were drawing large salaries but were not innovative or productive. They could be relied on to tell him whatever they felt he wanted to hear, which made his task of getting the company back into the black all the more difficult.

Ada had been honest about telling him what she thought the company needed: research and development, training for middle level management, targeted marketing and new markets. He remembered how she'd looked earlier that evening as he drove her home. Those large doe eyes, fringed with the longest eyelashes possible on any woman. That heart-shaped face with its generous mouth, and the delightful laugh she had. Her accent was musical, with a faint Igbo intonation, which he preferred to someone trying to mimic the Queen's English. The top two buttons on her emerald cotton blouse had been open, revealing her long, elegant neck. Most of the time she had been talking he had been fighting temptation and, when she started fiddling with the door, he should have just pressed the remote control but he had reached across her instead – and that had been his undoing. He had smelled the faint scent of her perfume and seen himself mirrored in her eyes. He had wanted to reach down and capture those beautiful lips with his own more than he had wanted anything else for a long time.

What is wrong with you? He had enough on his plate and yet all he could think about was Ada Okafor. He closed his eyes. This wouldn't do. He could not allow himself to be distracted by the charms and delights of accounts clerks – even if their smiles had the ability to rob him of intelligent thought.

Whenever they were in the same room an irresistible force seemed to pull him to her. He didn't know what it was. Except that, the more he saw of her, the more he wanted to know about her.

Ever since he'd taken up his new position in the company, he found himself going to the accounts department on the slightest pretext – just to catch a glimpse of Ada. He had been there eight times in the last two months. The last time he'd gone, Mrs Oseni had been quite surprised that he had found time to pop in for a 'chat'. He would pass Ada's desk each time. Sometimes she would look up and greet him and other times she seemed too busy to notice anything around her.

He opened the French windows and went back into his sitting room, which he jokingly referred to as the Oval Office because of its shape. It faced the garden and the lights surrounding the small swimming pool outside bounced off the water and reflected onto the windows. The walls were cream with wood panelling on alternate walls and there was a reddish-brown terracotta rug in the middle of the room, upon which stood a glass coffee table with a copy of *GQ* magazine on top of it. The large mustard-gold sofa was topped with wine-coloured linen cushions. A gigantic wall-mounted TV set dominated the room, with a minibar with assorted wines, beers and soft drinks below. The bar was mostly for entertaining, though. He was not much of a drinker. If he could not control his destiny, he would at least control himself.

He went into his study and looked around. The room

doubled as a library and books lined the long wall in several floor-to-ceiling bookshelves. The only other pieces of furniture were a desk littered with papers and books, a plush office chair and a state-of-the-art PC and printer.

He switched on the computer, looked at the screen and scrolled down.

"He had explored the land of pain – and was very familiar with every bit of its terrain. It no longer held any fear. As he lay on the cold road, rapidly crimsoning with the remnants of his life, his last thought was of his daughter, waiting at school for him to pick her up …"

He was stuck. He had been trying to move beyond this character … this chapter, but it wasn't flowing. Something was blocking his creativity and he didn't know what it was exactly – though there were quite a few things he could choose from.

Maybe I should leave the whole thing for now, he thought. He had a business to run and so many things competing for his attention, but he couldn't shake it. There was something in him, something deep within him, like an addiction, that needed to be fed. Back in London, the tutor at his evening writing class had told him that he had talent, so he had sent her the first three chapters of the novel he had been working on for the past five years. She had raved about it and told him to send her the whole book.

He had been working on it when he'd got the summons

from home to report to headquarters. Now, he was needed at City Finance. And with his dad's poor health, he had no other option.

So, he had to close the door on these intruding thoughts about Ada from accounts, and on his dream to be an author.

He had to look to his future.

His eyes settled on the glossy photograph of a beautiful woman dressed in a white and silver ball gown in a gold picture frame on his desk. She was tall and fair-skinned and her long hair fell in soft waves over her bare shoulders.

Gloria Onwuka. His long-term girlfriend and fiancée. The woman he was going to pledge his life to in a year's time.

That was, if she ever had the time to return his calls. He picked up his mobile, his hands hovering over the keys, then he shook his head and dialled her number and listened as it went into voicemail.

Hello. You've reached the voicemail of Gloria Onwuka. I can't take your call at the moment but if you would like to leave a message, I will definitely get back to you.

His lips tightened. He had left several messages that week and none had been answered. He put down the phone.

There was always tomorrow.

Six

Life went on as normal for Ada. A month passed by and she got on with her work and her studies. The end-of-term results were announced and she had performed well. Ada and Liz celebrated by going out for suya.

A week after her results, her brother Fred came to see her. At first, she was happy to see him, but when they spoke she found herself getting drawn into a familiar argument with him.

"You can't drop out of university, Fred," Ada said, fighting to control her anger.

"You don't understand, Sis. I need money. I can't keep on studying with no money. I need money to complete my projects and money to eat," he drawled. "A friend of mine suggested I try this American visa lottery thing."

Her brother was tall and gangly, a younger version of their father. *But without his wisdom and understanding*, Ada thought.

"Sense is not speaking to you, eh?" Ada spoke in Igbo. "You've spent three years in university and, with one more year to go, you want to leave it all and go to America – without a degree!" She was shouting now. "Are you sure that you have not been bewitched?"

"You see, I knew you wouldn't understand," Fred said, shaking his head. "Anyway, I am a man now. I need to sort out my own life."

"If you want to sort out your own life, go and finish your degree and help support Papa. 'Books: call Ada'. 'Money: call Ada'. 'The roof is falling down: call Ada'. How many pieces do you want me to divide myself into?"

Her brother said something under his breath, his tone harsh.

"Frederick Okafor! Did you just call me selfish?" Ada was furious now. She gestured around her room. "See this room … is this the room of someone who has all the money in the world, eh? Tell me?"

"Then marry someone and let him take care of you."

Ada had to restrain herself from slapping him. The last time she had gone home, a few months before Christmas, she had met one of her father's neighbours who had come to their house to pay their father his respects. He was a rich man and owned a bakery in a neighbouring town. Soon after, Auntie Alice, her father's sister, began writing her letters begging her to consider the baker as a suitor. Ada had laughed it off, as the man was closer in age to her father. Her father hadn't been impressed either and had told her not to worry about it. She certainly wasn't worried about it. She was incensed that it was even an issue.

"Auntie Alice was saying that in her day, a girl like you would marry the first suitor that came along to support her siblings and uphold her family's honour," Fred continued. "She wouldn't let her father's dilapidated house become a source of ridicule in the village. Ike ka e ji-añuogwu –

destitution breeds disdain. We can't even hold our heads up in our village because of our situation."

"Eh, so you won't be satisfied until I prostitute myself?" Ada asked. "If you don't like the situation, do something about it. Concentrate on graduating and getting yourself a good job so you can take care of Papa and look after the house. I can't do everything! I'm tired, you hear?"

In the end, Fred had made a kind of apology and eaten the meal of eba and bitter leaf soup she had made. Shortly afterwards he left to stay with his friend in Mushin before he went back to university in Nsukka.

She had a little money to spare and she gave it to him for his transport fare.

"Please think of Papa. Don't disgrace us, Fred," she told him before he left. "Finish your degree."

She was still thinking about her brother's visit when she got in to work the next day and saw Agatha and one of the women from the marketing department deep in conversation.

Agatha looked up as she walked in and they exchanged greetings.

"Are you here today?"

Ada nodded and she sat down.

Agatha turned to the other woman. "Ada is going to university you know. Na real Acada girl. When she isn't in accounts she works here on reception."

Ada felt two sets of eyes on her, sizing her up.

Then they started talking again. Ada switched on

the computer and saw that she had several emails. She scanned through them while the two women continued their conversation.

"You think say that your Oga in marketing dey on that list."

"I no know o. E be like say dem go keep am."

"I don tell my Oga at home, to prepare himself. Anything can happen o."

Ada heard a lull in the conversation and looked up to see Tony Okoli walking into the building with two businessmen carrying briefcases. From their accent she could hear that they were American.

Ada noticed that Tony Okoli wore a dark, tailored suit, and that he had a moustache now. It made him look even more dashing. Deep in conversation, the three men walked past and got into the lift. Ada tried to quash the feelings of disappointment that welled up within her. Tony hadn't even glanced in her direction. Ever since he had given her a lift – a month ago – they had hardly talked, except for the odd polite greeting now and then. He always seemed to be in a hurry.

Why do I feel as if we have some kind of connection when I don't even really know this guy? I've only spoken to him about three times, she chided herself. *Maybe I read too much into our friendly banter? Maybe it was all a bit of harmless flirting on his part?* Maybe she would never know.

That day he'd given her a lift back home, maybe she had misread everything else but she knew she hadn't misread the depth of the heat in his eyes as he'd touched her face.

She stared up at his back, admiring his broad shoulders for a moment. Then she looked away, back to her work on the computer.

It was the same with all these rich boys. Flirtation was one of their hobbies. She wasn't going let anyone play around with her like that.

***

Tony smiled as the meeting ended and the visitors were shown out. He turned to his director. "Mr Johnson, Standard Chartered and Barclays have shown some interest. I've got research and development looking into it. A lot of people are keen to get a piece of the emerging African market. We have to capitalise on that."

"I've got my project officer looking into it," Mr Johnson replied.

"Great. If I could have that report before the next board meeting."

There was a knock on the door and Mrs Oseni put her head into the meeting room.

"Just wanted to discuss the issue of middle-level management trainees."

Tony nodded as Mr Johnson took his leave.

"You asked all heads of departments to suggest possible candidates. Well, I've selected mine and I wanted to discuss it with you," Mrs Oseni stated.

"Yeah. Just e-mail the names to the management team. We'll be meeting in a few weeks' time and decisions will be made then."

"OK."

It wasn't until later that evening when he was catching up with his e-mails that Tony realised that Mrs Oseni had nominated Ada as one of the accounts team's candidates for trainee manager.

His lips curved into a smile. Girl Power. He had no problem with that. Looking at the company's most recent annual report, it looked as if the departments headed by women had the highest level of productivity. Ada had his vote any day, but, in the end, it would be up to Mrs Oseni and Ada's direct line manager to justify her nomination to the board and management team.

Thinking about Ada brought her face to mind again. Large expressive eyes full of an intensity that ignited something in him, her words echoing round his head.

"If any man is expecting any woman to double as cook, nanny, and dutiful daughter-in-law to all his relatives in today's world he might as well go marry a robot."

He smiled to himself and shook his head.

There was a woman who knew what she wanted out of life. He wished he was that certain.

***

Two weeks later, Ada was working late and humming along to P-Square's song 'No One Like You'. The office was empty. Even though her exams were now over, she continued to work well into the evening, often volunteering to work late so that she could get some overtime pay. It wasn't something that a lot of Nigerian companies allowed, but City Finance encouraged it and she was thankful for the opportunity to top up her wages.

She remembered the article on Tony Okoli that she had seen earlier that day in the gossip and society magazine *Lagos Now*, which Olu had left on her desk. It had a picture of Tony, dressed in a blue and white dashiki and a dashing white cap, casually lounging next to a sports car, on its cover.

She learned that he was 28. He liked sports cars, travelling and reading African literature, and wanted to make sure that City Finance continued to be a successful and thriving business.

Great picture. Mind-numbing, boring article. One of the reasons she never liked reading these magazines.

She continued humming the song to herself. Then, to her dismay, she saw Mr Obi.

See me see trouble o, she thought.

Standing in front of her desk, he seemed to glow with the triumph of finding her alone.

"Can I help you?" Ada's voice was as hard as concrete.

"That is a good question," he said, laughing.

"Mr Obi, I'm really busy at the moment."

"Work, work … that's all you know," he said. "You don't even know how to enjoy yourself." He leaned over her shoulder, bringing his face close to hers. She could smell the alcohol he had fortified himself with.

He moved around her desk, looming over her. "You think you are so special, don't you?" He reached down and grabbed her arm.

"Are you crazy?" Ada tried to push him away, which made his grip on her arm intensify, and he lunged, half-pushing, half-pulling her to the floor, scattering her files.

She screamed and tried to push him off but he was too strong. The alcohol seemed to have given him added strength. He began to fumble at her clothes.

His breath was hot against her neck. "You are so beautiful … I can't stop thinking about you …"

This can't be happening. This can't be happening, she kept telling herself. She stopped struggling for a moment, a move that he took as acquiescence.

"I like you, Ada. Why do you like to give me such a hard time, eh? I can put in a good word for you – at this time when they are getting rid of people, you need to be nice to someone like me."

She was filled with hatred for him. She jerked her left knee into his groin with a quick, sharp movement. His shout of pain echoed around the empty office.

She rolled away and scrambled to her feet, running to the door. Just as she reached the door, it burst open and she saw Tony Okoli standing in the doorway. He towered above her like an avenging angel, his eyes widening in shock. He took in the scene: Ada with her dishevelled hair and clothes and Mr Obi, who was still kneeling on the floor, groaning.

"What on earth is going on here?" Tony demanded.

Mr Obi stood up unsteadily, holding the edge of the desk to support himself.

"Oga, good … good evening, sir," he managed to say.

Tony walked over to where Mr Obi was and grabbed him by the collar of his shirt and slammed him against the wall.

"It's not what you think … she's my girlfriend …" Mr Obi stammered, with a sickly smile. "You are a man of the world. I'm sure you understand – this is just a lover's quarrel."

"And this is how lovers behave, eh? They attack the ones they love?" Tony looked like he wanted to punch the man. "Ada, are you OK?" Tony's eyes met hers and she nodded.

Tony faced Mr Obi again. "You had better start explaining what you think you were doing before I call the police."

"Oga …" Mr Obi started to tremble and wring his hands like some kind of demented creature. "This is not a police matter o. Me and Ada … we are …"

"We are what?" Ada shouted, glaring at him. "As if I would ever let such a person get anywhere near me! You are a liar and a disgrace, Mr Obi. Efulefu! Useless man."

"She has been giving me the green light – that's why I came to see her tonight." Mr Obi tried a begging tone. "Maybe I might have been a bit rough, but it was a slight mistake on my part. A small misunderstanding."

"Mr Obi, you are a complete disgrace to yourself and to our organisation," Tony hissed venomously.

Ada watched while Tony held Mr Obi down, and dialled a number on his mobile. "Security! Could you send up two men to the third floor? Accounts department. Yes. Just next to the lifts. We will be waiting."

Ada manoeuvred herself into a chair and stared at what was going on blankly.

"Ada – there are some security men coming up. Do you want to go to the Ladies'? You can tidy yourself up. You don't need to be here when they come in."

She nodded gratefully and left the room, trying her best to avoid the pleading look in Mr Obi's eyes. She made her way into the ladies' toilet opposite, and stared into the mirror. Soon she heard low voices, someone shouting, and then footsteps echoing down the hall.

She tried to analyse the events that had just taken place and what lay in front of her.

She would have to go to the police station and deal with all the bureaucracy, and then there were the policemen who would leer at her and ask her stupid questions.

Na your fault, now! You must have done something to make the man jump on you like that. You girls of nowadays. You no dey listen. You go dey wear small dress and then you go dey begin to hala if man look at you. Nonsense! You sure say dis man no be your boyfrien'?

Nothing would come out of it. Just more visits to the

police station, which would require bribing one of the officers or the DPO just to get Mr Obi charged. Her case would probably never get to court – and, even if it did, it would be her word against his. Her name would be in the papers and the shame of it would reach her hometown. Her reputation would be in ruins.

She heard Tony's concerned voice calling her name.

"Ada. I'm coming in. Are you OK?"

She was silent. Then the door opened slowly and Tony walked in.

"Are you alright?" he asked, clearly unnerved by her stillness.

She still didn't answer and he gently led her out of the toilet back into the office and pulled out a chair for her to sit on.

Ada looked down at herself. Her blouse was torn and she tried to cover herself, turning away from Tony's concerned gaze.

"Are you sure you are alright?" Tony asked again. He lowered his voice. "He didn't …"

She shook her head vehemently. "I'm fine."

She saw his face relax in relief.

"That's good. Would you like a cup of tea?"

She stared at him. Why on earth would she want to drink tea when she had just been assaulted?

"Silly me … sometimes I forget that I'm not in England anymore." He shook his head with a small smile, and then he was serious again. "It's OK, Ada. The authorities will deal with him."

She was silent for a time.

"I don't want to press charges," she finally said.

His eyes narrowed. "You what?"

"I can't cope with police trouble. You don't understand what it's like to go to the police with this kind of complaint."

"I saw Mr Obi attack you. I can back you up if you want."

"You don't understand. This isn't London. My reputation would be dragged into the mud because of that evil man. It would kill my father."

"I understand you don't want the publicity, but a lot of times men like him go free because women don't want to make a fuss. I know it's all raw and fresh right now, but why don't you go home and think it over? You might feel differently tomorrow. I'll – I mean the company will support you all the way."

"You have no idea what you are asking me to do," she said, sighing. "If I press charges, all of my business will be out on the road for people to use as a toothpick. Do you really think that having that fool taken to court is worth the damage it would do to me – and my reputation in this company? People will be pointing at me and saying 'Look at her, she must have done something – encouraged him somehow – for him to try to rape her.' I won't ever be able to shake it."

She felt tears welling up and, suddenly, she just wanted

to be as far away from the office as possible. "I just want to get out of here."

"Of course." He took off his jacket and handed it to her, taking care not to look at her torn clothes. "It wouldn't do for anybody to see you like this."

She put it on gratefully.

"How do you normally get home?"

"I take a bus."

He looked at his watch. "It's 8pm. Can't you take a taxi?"

She stared at him as if he was from another planet. "This is Lagos. It's not safe to take a taxi at this time of night." There were more passengers in buses and less chance of ending up in some bush, robbed, beaten up or worse. Besides she could not afford a taxi, but she wasn't going to tell him that. "I can take a molue."

"I couldn't possibly let you do that. I can take you home."

"Look, thanks for your help, but I'm OK. I probably know more about keeping myself safe in this city than you do."

"I really must insist, Ada."

She wanted to protest, but she saw his face and realised that he was not going to take no for an answer. Besides, her head felt as if someone was using it for football practice and she couldn't stop trembling. She nodded and got up – and almost collapsed – but his firm arm around her waist kept her upright.

"It's just shock," Tony said reassuringly. "Come on. We'll take the lift down to the ground floor. My car is parked at the entrance."

This time the dam burst and she began to cry, tears running down her face.

"Ada, don't cry. It's alright."

Tony rummaged in his pocket for a handkerchief, which he handed to her.

"I hate him. He makes me sick to the stomach. I can't stand working with him …"

Ada knew she was babbling and could hardly understand her own words, but Tony's deep reassuring voice soothed her. He gently led her out of the office to the lifts.

Seven

The next day, when Tony walked into the City Finance foyer, he couldn't believe his eyes. Ada Okafor was at reception, fielding the phones along with Agatha. Ada looked up and, when her eyes met his, he gave her a quizzical look as if to say: *Are you alright?* but she quickly looked away. From nowhere, an intense anger gripped at him and he strode towards the two ladies. Just as he reached the reception desk, the phone rang and he noticed Ada's hands were shaking as she picked it up. He greeted Agatha while he waited for Ada to finish her call. He was fuming.

"The meeting in the Atlantis meeting room?" Ada's voice was unsteady. "Sorry, Mr Oni, I forgot to book it. I will make sure it's done now. Yes. I'm so sorry ..."

Tony's face hardened. Ada, who was always so efficient, seemed all over the place today. She should not be at work.

"May I help you, sir?" She was finally off the phone. Her red eyes spoke of a sleepless night filled with nightmares – and he knew why. He frowned. *Not good.* He shook his head and headed for his office without a word.

***

Tony worried about Ada all morning. The image of her face as she'd wept was imprinted on his memory. Finally, he had called down to reception to check on her.

"Ada?"

"Yes, sir?"

"Have you gone to lunch yet?"

"No." Her voice sounded hesitant, but over the phone he couldn't be sure.

"It's almost 2pm," he said.

"Do you want me to do something for you, sir?"

"Go for your lunch break and come up and see me at 2.30pm."

"Yes, sir."

While Tony waited, he checked his e-mails and made a few phone calls. But he was edgy and irritable. He had already upset his secretary when he lost his temper because she couldn't find a letter she was meant to have filed.

Finally, at 2.30pm, there was a knock on the door and Ada opened the door. She stood there hesitantly.

"Ada, please come in." Tony said. "Sit down."

She shut the door and took a seat in front of his desk. At another time she would have registered that this was the first time she had been in his office. She noticed the large round steel table and matching chairs in the centre of the room, the expensive leather desk, the abstract painting on the wall and the view of the city from the large windows. Ada noticed that he had stood up when she came in, and was still standing.

"Ada … I wasn't expecting you to be at work today."

"Yes, well …" She didn't look at him, but fiddled with her hands in her lap. "I felt much better and decided to come in."

He studied her intently and sat down. She looked tired and drawn.

"I told you to ring Mrs Oseni or your supervisor and explain what happened. They would understand and I trust their discretion."

"I don't trust that easily."

"Fair enough, but I think you should take some time off. Speak to HR. You can cite stress and I'll back you up. You should be at home resting."

"I said I'm fine, sir." Her eyes narrowed and she was clearly battling to keep her emotions in check. "I just would like to move on."

"What happened to you is not something you can just 'move on' from." He spoke slowly. He knew that if he didn't he would start getting impatient with her, and she didn't need that now. "I would much rather you stay at home and recover properly than come in here pretending that everything is fine – like some sort of bloody robot."

She sprang up, pushing the chair back on the smooth polished floor with an angry scraping noise.

"I don't need you to dictate to me. It's my life and I take responsibility for my own decisions. I appreciate your help yesterday, sir, but it doesn't give you the right to play Dr Phil. You are my boss and not my father."

He looked at her and saw the resolution mixed with angry tension in her slight shoulders. He also saw the exhaustion and stress behind the hardness in her eyes. He noticed her hands were gripping the edge of the desk to steady herself and that they were shaking.

"Ada … are you alright?"

"Of course. May I go now?"

"I would like you to take the rest of the day off."

"I'm fine, sir."

"I insist. You can take it as a sick leave, compassionate leave or whatever. Take a few days off – Mrs Oseni will be informed and your work allocated to one of your colleagues."

Ada wanted to say no but he interrupted her.

"Ada, this is not up discussion."

Ada admitted some days off would be good. She couldn't concentrate on anything and felt close to tears every five minutes. But why was this guy so intent on bulldozing his way into her life? It was nice that someone cared about her welfare but was it the concern of an employer or something more? Then she saw that look in his eyes again. The same look he had when he had taken her home after Mr Obi's attack. Concern with a hint of kindness in those compelling eyes. Kindness that could make a woman go weak, especially if she had never known such a thing in past relationships.

Weakness was too expensive. Especially with someone like him. Rich, successful and charming. It could be her downfall. Maybe Tony Okoli and not Mr Obi was the real risk.

She nodded quietly. "Thank you."

"See you next week."

"OK."

He watched her leave, quietly closing the door behind her, and listened to her footsteps echoing down the corridor.

Okoli, what are you doing? Let her manager take care of it. Don't get involved.

Tony shook his head. He was already involved. In his head, in his heart. He was more involved than he had the right to be.

***

Ada was glad for the break and the weekend. She had no choice but to try to put what had happened to her to the back of her mind and concentrate on the future.

On Saturday she'd planned to go to the hairdresser, but decided against it and stayed at home. It was quiet as most of her neighbours had gone to social events, so she was spared from blaring music or people arguing.

She sat on her bed, about to start reading a book, when she was interrupted by her phone.

She picked it up and looked at the screen: an unknown number. "Hello?"

A deep, familiar voice answered. "Ada. Sorry to ring you like this but I – I mean – we wanted to find out how you were doing?"

Ada put down her book and ran a hand over her head, as her heartbeat quickened. Her mouth felt dry. "Who is this?" She knew who it was. So, why ask?

She heard Tony Okoli's deep laugh. "It's me, Ada. Tony."

It was her turn to laugh. *Ada. When Oga patapatas begin dey call you for house no be for play o.* "Hello, sir. I'm fine." She didn't even know when the *sir* slipped in. Maybe it was out of shock or the desire to maintain some distance between them.

Mr Obi had torn her clothes. Tony had been such a gentleman – turning away for her to put on his jacket to cover her modesty. She felt embarrassed by the little he had seen.

"How are you, Ada ? I've been thinking ... I mean I've been worried about you. Is someone looking after you?"

Even the way he said her name, the deep inflection in his voice when he asked after her wellbeing, touched her heart in more ways than she could express. No-one could sound that genuine unless they really cared.

Could they?

"My roommate is taking care of me."

There was a pause and then the voice was more formal. "OK then. That's put my mind at ease. Well, see you next week Ada."

"Thanks."

She ended the call and stood looking at the phone. Then she sighed and picked up her book.

Eight

On Monday morning Ada was back working in accounts.

She had just sat down at her desk and switched on her laptop, when …

"Oga dey look for you."

She turned round to see Olu staring at her, a pitying look on his face.

"Really?" Maybe that was why he called her. *He wants to soften the blow before the bad news.*

"They started on Thursday, a couple of days after you went on leave. Half of marketing have been given letters to go. Mr Coker, the head of HR, is leaving too. They started calling in people from accounts on Friday. I went to thanksgiving in my church yesterday. As you can see I still dey here thank God."

Her heart plummeted. *Oh no. The dreaded call from management.*

Olu saw her face and patted her on the shoulder. "Don't worry, Ada. I'm sure they will keep you. Everybody knows how hard you work."

She went to her inbox and saw the e-mail from her head of department. There was a meeting invite for 10am with the M.D.

Panic gripped her immediately and, when she had a moment to spare, she stumbled to the toilet and stared at her reflection in the mirror. She was wearing a simple white shirt and brown tailored skirt with medium heels; her long hair was tied in a ponytail. She hoped that she wasn't going to be one of the victims of the retrenchment exercise. It would be disastrous if that happened. She needed this job to pay her bills and her fees at university and continue to send money home to her father. Although she found it hard to admit it to herself, the thought of not bumping into Tony in the corridor, or seeing him breeze through reception or accounts, made her heart sink.

At just before 10am, Ada went to the executive suite on the management floor and knocked on the door.

"Come in," said a voice she couldn't identify.

She entered a large oval room. Ten chairs were arranged around a long glass table but there were only four people in the room: herself; Mrs Oseni, the head of accounts; her direct line manager, Mrs Solanke and Tony Okoli, who sat at the head of the table, looking straight at her.

Everyone looked very serious and formal.

"Ada, good to see you," said Mrs Oseni. "I hope you are much better now."

"Yes, much better, thank you, ma."

"Please sit down, Ada," Tony said, gesturing to a chair opposite him next to Mrs Solanke.

Their eyes met and for a second Ada forgot where she was. She felt as though it was just the two of them in this big room with the long table and lots of chairs. She saw the tenderness in his smile and felt reassured that everything was going to be alright.

Mrs Oseni interrupted her thoughts. "Good to have you back, Ada."

Tony cleared his throat. "We have been looking at your work and your attention to detail with our new suppliers' system. You have also been providing a professional service at reception. We are impressed that you have combined all this with your work at university. We would like to offer you a place on our new trainee management scheme."

She stared at the panel.

"Really?" she squeaked in surprise. "Wow, that's wonderful …" While her money problems were not necessarily over, it was a relief to know that she wasn't going to be homeless or unable to carry on with her degree.

There was a nod from the panel and Mrs Solanke, who was sitting closest to her, shook her hand.

"Congratulations, I think you can handle it," Mrs Oseni said, smiling. "You've got a good track record and we have no doubt that you will do really well. You are just the sort of employee that we value."

"Thank you. I really appreciate this opportunity," Ada said, adjusting herself to sit up straighter in her chair.

"You start in three months' time," Tony added. "A letter will be sent to confirm this offer."

"Thanks. Thank you so very much." Ada had to stop herself from screaming with delight. She left the room in a daze.

It was great news but she realised that Tony might have had something to do with it. She was grateful but cautious.

Just what is he expecting in exchange for this promotion?

But she decided to brush her concerns aside and try to enjoy her newfound success. Maybe she was being unfairly suspicious. It could just be that all her hard work was beginning to pay off at last.

***

That Saturday, Ada took Liz to Chicken Republic in VI to celebrate. It was a great feeling to finally be able to treat her roommate. Liz had been such a support to her over the past couple of years – ever since she had moved to Lagos.

"Well, you are definitely going up in the world," Liz said, sipping her Fanta.

"I haven't started yet. The next scheme starts in September. That's still about three months away."

"I'm sure your Mr Okoli had something to do with it," Liz teased.

"He is not 'my Mr Okoli', biko. All he did was to approve my boss's application."

"Yes, but he could have said no."

"Well, he didn't. Do you want another doughnut?"

"I've had two already," Liz said. "Ada, why are you always so defensive every time I bring up Tony Okoli?"

"He is my boss."

"That is not what I asked you. E be like say you like this man o."

Ada got up and pushed back her chair. "I'm going to get some meat pies. Do you want another Fanta?"

Liz shook her head and laughed. "I think you really *do* like this man."

Ada pretended not to hear her last comment but, as she joined the queue of customers waiting to be served, she realised that, when it came to Tony Okoli, she felt a strong sense of attraction, which she wasn't ready to admit – even to herself. And, while the attraction filled her with a heady sense of exhilaration and excitement, it also made her feel vulnerable, something she didn't like at all.

***

"Sometimes I feel as if I'm going to implode."

Tony was sitting on the balcony of the Golden Palm Resort and Hotel with his best friend Richard, soaking in the fresh air. It was the newest hang-out spot for the Lekki yuppies and he hated it. He was there because of Richard.

He hated the pseudo-American atmosphere of the place, he hated the noise, and, above all, he hated the self-absorbed yuppies chatting loudly in their fake American accents about their latest holiday in Dubai or their shopping trip in Miami. He detested having to listen to them go on and on about their executive jobs that their popsies had 'worked' for them in top banks or foreign companies, or their 'pads' – an American word he disliked intensely – in Lekki, Ikoyi and VGC. Flaunting their wealth with expensive clothes, cars and lifestyles but hating them was like hating himself; their lives were a mirror of his own.

The waiting staff were the picture of busy efficiency in the way they served the loudmouth yuppies. Usher's latest number *Caught Up* boomed out of the speakers.

The food made up for it, though. There was hot beef, chicken and seafood suya, steak, pasta, pizza, cocktails and a full wine list. They even had a happy hour for those who wanted to drink themselves silly.

"I'm sorry, man," Richard said, shaking his head. "I didn't know you were under that much pressure."

Richard Balogun, childhood school friend, partner in crime and confidant, was a tall, dark bespectacled lawyer, now slightly balding. His killer instinct in the courtroom was a direct contrast to the fact that he was a softie at heart, especially when it came to his wife Kunbi, and their two children. He and Tony had kept in touch over the years, even after Tony had gone to England for his education.

"I can understand why Dad had to take a back seat," Tony continued. "Sometimes I find myself staying up into the early hours of the morning, replying to e-mails, going through plans, proposals and contracts – trying to figure out how to keep this company afloat. The livelihoods of almost a hundred people are depending on me."

A smiling waiter came up with a tray of smoking-hot beef suya, the savoury, peppery smell tickling his nostrils and momentarily distracting him from his train of thought.

"Make una try this suya," Richard suggested, "They say it's even better than Obalende suya."

Tony picked up a piece of hot meat and munched away.

He looked out over the sea, a shimmering green-blue expanse of unending possibility. Unlike his future. Then his old friend's voice broke into his thoughts.

"So, what's going on with you and Gloria now?"

"She is coming over in a couple of weeks. It's her old man's 60th birthday," Tony said, sighing.

"You don't exactly sound excited."

"I don't know, Richard. I don't think this long-distance thing is working." He stared at the young couple walking across the way, hand in hand. "Sometimes we can go for weeks without talking to each other, and then we use work as an excuse. We haven't really spoken in ages. I mean, really been real with each other. When I bring this up, she just gets defensive."

"Don't worry, when she comes just go away for a weekend and rekindle the old fire." Richard grinned mischievously. "There is this holiday resort – fantastic little chalets with all the amenities around Kuramo Waters. My boss recommended it. Kunbi and I went there for our honeymoon. Let's just say it was a holiday we still remember – two kids and five years of domesticity later."

"Really?" Tony looked wryly. He and Gloria hadn't even started gathering the wood for the fire, let alone rekindling it. Besides, lately, the only fire in his blood was for Ada, and the reality of that was alarming. Gloria would be coming home soon. They had a lot to sort out and adding his feelings for Ada into the equation made things even more complicated.

He stared into his glass. Coke on the rocks with lemon, a large dose of introspection and a splitting headache. He lifted his head and looked at his childhood friend.

"I'm going to head back home soon. Got a terrible headache and this music isn't helping."

"Party pooper," Richard said, laughing. "Knowing you, it's probably straight to bed with a book or something. Speaking of books, you were talking of writing one, last time we met up in London. How far are you with that?"

"It's coming along," Tony smiled. "Slowly but surely."

"Huh? What's that supposed to mean?"

"It's a long story, man, one that I'm too tired to tell right now. Hey, I can hear your kids calling for their daddy. Let's go. I can't leave you here with these runs girls and yuppies. Kunbi would never forgive me."

Richard groaned and got up slowly. "Party pooper."

Nine

A week later Ada was in the canteen when she saw Tony Okoli walking towards her carrying a plate of beans and plantain on a tray. Suddenly she was very conscious of herself. She was glad that she had worn a smart new blouse and skirt that day and that instead of pinning her braids up, she was wearing them down, framing her face in a long, stylish bob.

He stopped when he reached her and smiled. "Hello, Ada. How are you?"

"I'm quite well, thank you."

"Mind if I join you?"

"Of course not."

He pulled out a chair and sat down opposite her.

"You will be starting your training soon, won't you?" Ada nodded. Tony picked up the salt shaker on the table and began to season his food.

She looked past Tony and caught Agatha's cool glance from a few tables away. A few others sat eating with their eyes fixed on them.

Ada resolved to ignore the stares. *Who are they to presume whom she could talk to anyway?* She turned her attention back to the man opposite her.

She watched him put his fork into the food and begin to eat. She noticed his grimace at the taste and she bowed her head so he wouldn't see her smile.

"So, read any more good books lately?" she asked.

"I'm reading Cyprian Ekwensi's *Jagua Nana*."

"I haven't really read him. I'm more of an Achebe fan."

He shook her head. "They are both great writers. You know he wrote quite a few books, right? This one is about a Nigerian woman struggling for equality and wealth in a Nigerian society that was not quite ready for her."

"When is it set?"

"In the sixties."

"Hmmm. Sounds interesting."

They continued to eat in silence.

"So what are you reading now?"

"*Joys of Motherhood*."

"Ah, Buchi Emecheta. I really like her writing. She has a way of getting inside what women really face in our culture."

She was glad to hear that he not only knew her, but got her. "I'm in a book club and that's the book we are looking at this month ..."

"A book club?" He seemed excited.

"It's great and it's just around the corner, not too far from Apongbon Street. We meet for an hour at 12 noon every fortnight. Sometimes, I just get a snack from the eatery next door and go. "

"Sounds like my kind of thing. When is the next one?"

"Next Wednesday. You can come if you like ..." She saw the surprised look on his face and immediately wished she could take the words back. "Don't mind me.

I'm sure you are terribly busy – clients, meetings and all kinds of stuff."

"Not at all … that sounds great," he said and smiled a slow smile that brought out the dimple on his left cheek.

She felt her stomach twist into knots. *Don't smile at me like that. It makes me go to pieces and I need to keep myself together. Especially when I'm around you.*

"Sometime when I'm not terribly busy – when I don't have clients to take out to lunch, meetings or whatever – I might just pop in. Or maybe we could meet up earlier and then go together."

Ada picked up her glass of water and downed it in one gulp, almost choking in the process.

He looked concerned. "Are you OK?"

She nodded weakly. "I'm fine. The water just went down the wrong way."

They chatted a little while longer and then he looked at his watch.

"Well, that's me done," he said pushing his chair back. "Goodbye, Ada."

"Goodbye, Mr Okoli," she replied and he walked away. She turned back to her food.

She had only asked Mr Tony Okoli, the M.D. of City Finance, whether he might be interested in attending the nearby lunchtime book club. It wasn't a date or a secret meeting, so why was her heart racing and why did she feel as if the whole world had heard every word she had said?

Then Agatha slid into the chair opposite her, with eyes full of questions.

"Ah-ah … wetin dey happen now?" Agatha whispered conspiratorially. "All this talk-talk with Oga Junior abeg gist me."

"There is no gist, Agatha."

"Are you sure? This isn't the first time I've seen you people talking."

"Eh? So, when did talking to somebody become an offence?"

"When person dey begin to answer question with question, you know say somebody dey hide something be dat."

"Na you know, jare, Agatha. We were just discussing a novel that I was reading."

"Novel?" Agatha gave her a hard look. "Which novel?"

Ada had had enough. She got up from her chair. "*One Half of a Blue Sun.*"

Ada closed her eyes. Agatha hadn't even realised that no such book existed.

She picked up her tray and Agatha followed. "Na true be dat o? Let me have a look at it. You never know – posing with a book makes you look really cool, you know. Maybe I should try it during my next lunch break. There is one new guy in marketing and he looks really acada–ish you know …"

***

It was later that afternoon, when his meetings had been concluded for the day, that Tony allowed himself to play back what had taken place between Ada and him in the canteen.

She had invited him to her book club. While he liked the idea of talking to other people about his favourite subject, if he was honest with himself, he would be more interested in spending time with Ada alone, away from the goldfish bowl that was the office. Of course it could have just been a friendly suggestion on her part, which he could shrug off, but something deep down inside him felt it was much more.

It was up to him to make the next move.

***

Ada was working in accounts. She heard the familiar ping of another e-mail landing in her inbox and looked up. Her mouth went dry.

Tony Okoli had sent her an e-mail!

He didn't turn up after their hasty arrangement to go to the book club together a week ago. Disappointed and feeling a bit silly, she had shrugged it off and now this ...

Her heart pounded as she scanned the contents.

```
From: Tony Okoli <tonyokoli@cityfinance.com>
Date: Tuesday, 13 October 2009 10.00
To: Ada Okafor <adaokafor@cityfinance.com>
Subject: Re: Art Exhibition
```

```
Hi Ada,
Hope you are well. Terribly sorry couldn't
make book club but I have an invitation
for an opening this Friday evening and was
wondering whether you might be free?
It's an exhibition of paintings by famous
Nigerian artists.

Kind regards,

Tony
```

Is this a date? she wondered. Maybe it was just a casual thing – between two people who liked each other's company and shared the same interests? Or perhaps it was some kind of intricate plot to get her alone so he could try something – her experience with Mr Obi was never far from her mind. She shut out the conflicting voices in her head and typed out a reply:

```
Date: Tuesday, 13 October 2009 10.20
From: Ada Okafor <adaokafor@cityfinance.
com>
To: Tony Okoli <tonyokoli@cityfinance.com>
Subject: Re: Art Exhibition

Dear Tony,

Thanks for the invite. It sounds very
interesting and I would love to attend.

Regards,

Ada
```

Her finger hovered over the send button. *Too familiar.* *Too eager.* She didn't want him to think that she was reading more into the invite than he intended. She deleted what she had written and tried again:

```
Date: Tuesday, 13 October 2009 10.30
From: Ada Okafor <adaokafor@cityfinance.
com>
To: Tony Okoli <tonyokoli@cityfinance.com>
Subject: Re: Art Exhibition

Dear Mr Okoli,

Many thanks for your invite. I accept
your invitation and look forward to this
prestigious event.

Yours sincerely,

A Okafor
```

Way too formal. It sounded like typical bureaucratic speak from the Government Secretariat at Alausa.

The matter was beginning to bite into her working time, so she decided on something more concise: not too formal and not too familiar.

```
Date: Tuesday, 13 October 2009 10.40
From: Ada Okafor <adaokafor@cityfinance.
com>
To: Tony Okoli <tonyokoli@cityfinance.com>
Subject: Re: Art Exhibition
```

```
Thanks for the invite, Tony. Look forward
to meeting up.

Regards

Ada Okafor
```

She pressed send. That should have been the end of it.
But she kept turning it over in her mind, bringing it out to
ruminate and dissect and then push back to the recesses
of her head. She decided to keep the invitation to herself.
If this piece of information got out into the public domain
she would live to regret it.

An hour later she got a reply, short and succinct.

```
From:  Tony  Okoli  <tonyokoli@cityfinance.
com>
Date: Tuesday, 13 October 2009 11.40
To: Ada Okafor <adaokafor@cityfinance.com>
Subject: Re: Art Exhibition

Great! Will come and pick you up at home
around 8pm.

Tony.
```

By the end of the week she had completely rationalised
the matter. She was going to play it cool. The e-mail had
been casually polite so she would act accordingly: casual
and polite.

Ten

Tony arrived to pick her up at 8pm. She appeared wearing a simple sleeveless knee-length dress made of brown ankara print, patterned with green leaves. A green belt and matching heels gave her some added height. Her braids were pulled back high on her forehead, her eyes had a mysterious look, and a large gold hoop earrings hung from her ears.

I like. Very much, Tony thought to himself when he saw her at her gate. *Maybe too much.*

"Good evening, Ada," he said when she got into the car. "You look nice." That wasn't what he wanted to say, though.

Ada, you look drop-dead gorgeous. Utterly alluring.

His eyes lingered on her for a minute more.

Then he looked up. She was looking at him curiously.

"How was your day?"

His face assumed its usual easy, friendly look. "Brilliant." He put the key in the ignition and they were off.

When they arrived, the exhibition halls were packed with people, some standing alone, others in groups discussing the paintings. As it was a corporate affair, most of them were smartly dressed in suits and dresses. The rest of the people were clearly artists wearing jeans, T-shirts and dreadlocks. Some stewards in white shirts and black trousers served soft drinks, wine and canapés.

There were charcoal drawings, pencil drawings and oil paintings on display. Some were abstract and others depicted everyday scenes, a busy market, Lagos during rush hour, two kids playing in a stream, some women dressed in white garments attending a church service on a busy beach.

They strolled through the gallery, discussing the merits of the different works. They stopped for a while to listen to a lecturer telling the visitors about the artists and their works.

"I would like to buy a piece for my sitting room. It looks so bare," Tony said as they walked. "But I know so little about African art, you see. I have some ideas, but I'm not sure, so I need someone with taste to guide me."

"What about that one?" Ada asked, nodding towards an oil painting of a bustling market scene.

"It's nice," Tony said, nodding. "I can see it in my study."

"I like the way the light is falling on the people's faces." She pointed at one of the people in the scene, a little girl selling oranges under the shade of a tree. Eating alone, with a small smile on her face, she looked joyful. "It's got character." Ada said, "But it's also got a million naira price tag."

Ada's comment settled it for him. "I'll take it."

"It's a good choice," Ada murmured. Her mind was doing some quick calculations. She couldn't help it. A million was just below her annual salary. A year's salary just for one picture! Whoever said having money didn't make life easier ...

"Are you hungry?" Tony asked after he had finished negotiating with the gallery owner and the picture had been wrapped up and handed over. "I know I am."

"Yes ..." She wasn't sure how to respond.

"We can have dinner at my place."

She stared at him.

"Dinner ..."

"Yes, dinner. Then you can have a look at my collection as well."

"Collection?"

"Of diamonds and rare stones."

"Are you making fun of me?"

"My books," he said, laughing. "They are more precious to me than gold or jewels. I have a whole study of them – wall to wall. I'd be happy to lend some to you, if you like."

She nodded and pushed aside the voice of experience and common sense.

How well do you even know this guy? He is your boss but you never know ...

***

Ada was impressed as they sped past the well-lit gardens and houses of the rich. She knew that these homes cost millions of dollars. She wondered what it would be like to live in an area like this with a staff of cooks, gardeners and house helps to do whatever you wanted, whenever you wanted to do it.

She also wondered whether this man, whom she was beginning to like lot, had such an army in his house.

His house was a two-bedroomed affair with a modest garden on a quiet street and a solitary security guard who saluted when they drove in. He parked his car in the garage and they walked a few yards to the house.

Ada expected a full complement of servants to come out of the house. But no one came and Tony let himself into the building.

He switched on the light to reveal a large room with French windows that overlooked the garden. The walls were cream and the long leather sofa was the colour of warm gold. There were plants everywhere, large dark-green palms that made her feel as if she was in the middle of a forest.

Everything was so clean and orderly and spacious.

Tony picked up the remote and the massive wall-mounted TV flickered to life.

"Can I get you a drink? Tea, coffee – or something stronger?"

"I don't drink." She tried not to sound apologetic, not wanting him to think she was a naïve bush girl.

"Another thing we have in common," he said, smiling.

He went to the bar and opened what looked like a cupboard until she realised it was in a fridge built into the wall. "Some fruit juice, then?"

"Yes, please."

He produced a carton of orange and mango juice, poured some into a glass and handed it to her.

"Do make yourself at home. I don't often have visitors, so it's always nice to have someone round to have intelligent conversation with …"

She looked around her, trying not to look too awed. She saw a swimming pool through the French windows. *Wow.* "It's a lovely place."

"It's one of my father's buildings – I need to keep reminding myself of that. I keep it simple. I like the clean, minimalist, uncluttered look. I can show you around the library if you like. Bring your drink."

She followed him into the next room. The first thing that struck her was the wall-to-wall shelves of books. He wasn't joking when he said it was a library. It looked as if this was his favourite place in the house. There was a comfortable-looking armchair next to a window that overlooked the garden and another chair at his desk.

She went to the books and ran through the titles.

Business and the State in Developing Countries, The 7 Habits of Highly Effective People, The Bible …

The Bible?

He didn't strike her as a person of faith. Not being devout herself, she hadn't thought to ask. All her faith had been buried with her mother in the central cemetery in her home town.

She moved to another shelf where she spotted some

fiction books – Jane Austen, Charles Dickens, J.D. Salinger, Ngũgĩ wa Thiong'o, Cyprian Ekwensi, Chinua Achebe – and picked one out. *Persuasion*.

"You do love sad love stories, don't you?" Tony's deep voice interrupted her thoughts. "First Pip and Estella in *Great Expectations* and now Captain Wentworth and Anne Elliot."

She laughed. "Abeg leave me jo. They got together in the end, didn't they?"

"Yep. Wentworth realised he didn't want to lose her. After all those years ... anyway, I have a lot of books waiting to be read ... someday."

She turned round and smiled. "It's a wonderful room."

"This is where I do a lot of my work," he said. "Let's get this picture up. You can tell me whether it suits the room."

He unwrapped the painting and held it against the wall. He liked the way the light picked up its rich earthy colours beautifully.

"Perfect," she said, almost to herself.

"I like it," he agreed. "Now, let's do something about dinner." She followed him into a gleaming white kitchen. Grey pebble-like tiles covered the floor and white hand-fired tiles lined the walls. There were modern fixtures everywhere: a stove with a built-in microwave above it and a gigantic American-style two-door fridge.

Very nice, she thought. *This is money talking.* "Could I use your bathroom please?"

He led her out of the kitchen and down a corridor with more paintings on the wall. The guest toilet was next to a wide flight of stairs going up to the first floor.

She closed the door behind her and shook her head in awe at the shining silver taps, water heater, air-conditioner, a soft and white hand towel. Even this guest toilet was worlds away from 25 Akinsanmi Street, where the toilet was a little fenced-off partition at the back of the yard.

She washed her hands and stood staring at her reflection in the mirror.

What on earth are you doing in your boss's house at nine o'clock on a Friday night? How many other women has he brought back to his house?

By the time she rejoined him in the kitchen she had collected her thoughts.

He turned to face her, and her heart beat faster at the broadness of his shoulders and his strong forearms, which she could see clearly now that he had rolled up his sleeves.

"Do you like Chinese?"

She nodded, trying to look composed.

He doesn't have to know that the last time I had a Chinese meal was last year when Mrs Oseni celebrated her 50th birthday at a posh hotel and invited the team.

She watched, puzzled, as he took out fresh vegetables and a bag of prawns from the freezer and put them on the kitchen counter.

Don't tell me this guy is expecting me to cook his dinner?

"I can rustle up some prawn fried rice, if you'd like?" he suggested.

"Yes, that would be nice." Then, to her delight, he brought out a chopping board and started peeling and slicing the vegetables. She watched his deft movements with the knife.

"Don't look so surprised. Some of us men know how to cook as well, you know."

She smiled guiltily, realising that he had just read her mind. A man who loved books, had a great sense of humour, and was handsome, kind and loaded, and who could cook as well. He must be too good to be true.

Maybe he is? Maybe any minute he is going to grow three heads and try something monstrous.

She sat down on one of the tall leather-backed stools in the dining area and watched him rinse some basmati rice and put it into a pot, before lightly frying the prawns.

"I studied abroad. If I hadn't learned how to cook, I'd have starved."

The aroma of spices assailed her senses and she turned her attention back to him as he fried the rice, spices, prawns and vegetables in a large pan, adding some soy sauce and stock cubes as he worked.

She watched him, mesmerised, aware that she could have sat there all night.

"Well done. You clearly know what you're doing in the kitchen."

"Thanks." He fetched two plates and served them and,

instead of eating in the large dining room, they took their plates to the sitting room and sat on the big, comfortable sofa.

"Wow, you are a great cook. This is delicious, Tony," Ada said, seemingly surprised.

"Thanks! I aim to please. So, Ada … what's next in your plan for world domination?"

"World domination? Of course not. I just want a good career, hopefully an MBA, and to make sure that my father is provided for."

"No ideas of love or meeting Mr Right? Isn't that the dream of all women?"

"Hardly. Thank God the days where marriage is the only option to avoid a life of poverty and disgrace are drawing to an end."

"OK, so your career is on track. Is marriage out of the question for you?

She shrugged. "Not if I meet the right man."

"Define the 'right man'?" he asked teasingly, his eyes resting on her face.

"My Mr Right would be someone who respects my opinion, who believes in me and supports my dreams and visions. A man who is strong and confident enough to allow me to grow and excel – even as I support him. A man who walks by my side, but doesn't coerce; a man who is gentle and kind, compassionate, tender and understanding."

"Wow … that's some list," Tony said, leaning back to

take a look at her. "Where do you think you are going to find this paragon of virtue?"

"I don't know … I'm not really looking for him right now."

He laughed at that. "Ada Okafor, I like you," he said suddenly.

She was at a loss for words and continued eating. He smiled again.

"And because I like you," he continued, "I'm going to tell you something about me that only a few people know."

Her heart raced. "And that is?"

"Give me a minute." He got up and left the room, leaving her to speculate feverishly on what the secret was.

He returned and handed her a bulky package. She had finished her food and was about to take her plate to the kitchen, but he took it from her.

When he came back from the kitchen, he sat on the sofa next to her.

"I'm working on a novel. Maybe when you have a moment … I'd really value your opinion."

She scanned through the manuscript and for a few minutes there was silence. Then she looked up and smiled.

"This looks interesting."

"I hope you aren't just saying that to spare my feelings. I've written some short stories as well. An editor in London is reading them."

"No, this is good. I would like to read it sometime – when I'm not studying that is."

"I forget you are still studying. I feel as if I'm taking you away from your studies for my own selfish reasons."

"And are your reasons selfish?"

He looked at her, his eyes exploring her face.

"Um hm. Right now, I think they are. Very selfish …"

She stared at him, seeing herself mirrored in his eyes. He was that close. She opened her mouth to ask him a question and she saw the hunger in his eyes, they rested on her lips.

"Ada …

He cupped her face in his hands and leaned in to capture her lips with his.

Hot blood pounded through his head. Maybe it was her lip gloss but she tasted the way he dreamed she would, like warm honey. His arms slipped around her slim waist to hold her closer. The soft, delicate curves of her body moulded against him, as if she had been created just for him.

Ada linked her arms around his shoulders and their kiss deepened and sensations shot through her veins like lightning. She felt his heart beating against hers. She couldn't believe he was kissing her like this but it felt so right.

He was the first to break away, his breath sounding heavy and laboured, his eyes travelling over her. She lay back against the sofa, staring at him, her lips still tingling.

"I can't do this …" she heard him say. His voice seemed to come from far away. "I must be mad, bringing you here like this …"

She saw the regret in his eyes as he backed away. A feeling of cold spread all over her and she was mortified and confused.

"Tony. What do you want from me?" she asked sharply.

He stood up and put a hand to his head as if thinking straight was difficult for him. "I had no right to let things go this far. You are a wonderful person and very attractive, but my life is like a roller-coaster at the moment and the last thing you need is for someone like me to complicate yours. I can't have a relationship with you – or anyone else."

"Who said I wanted a relationship with you anyway?" Ada said, her face set into a frown. She moved to the far end of the couch to create as much distance from him as possible. "You invited me here. You kissed me…"

"Ada, you're right and I'm really sorry," he said sighing. His voice took on the professional tone she recognised. "I should never have brought you here. It's not appropriate and it will never happen again."

"That's fine by me," Ada said, standing up. "I think it is best that I leave now."

"I think that will be best. Let me give you a lift home." Tony picked up his keys, but Ada shook her head.

"That won't be necessary. I can make my way home."

She was still dazed when she picked up her bag and walked out of the room. What was she thinking? She hadn't even pushed him away. Her mind projected forward to what might have happened if the kiss had progressed further. She might have joined the list of women who landed in his house. Used and discarded like toilet paper.

Mba. Not me. Not Ada Jennifer Okafor. No way.

She walked out of the door. He was standing in front of her in the passage to the front door, his eyes hooded. "Look, I may be an idiot but no way am I allowing you to take public transport from Ikoyi to Surulere at this time of the night."

She shrugged. "Have it your own way. I just want to leave."

He nodded.

Eleven

A week later, Tony was at Murtala Muhammed Airport in Lagos. He was sitting motionless in the arrivals hall, his head in his hands. He was oblivious to all the frenzied activity around him.

What have you done? He should never have kissed Ada. He had been asking himself this question ever since the night he had taken her back to his house. It was a mistake and he'd known it the minute he had invited her to the exhibition. Now he had messed everything up.

There was an announcement of a plane arriving from Washington and he got up and pushed through the crowd, mingling with family, friends and other well-wishers waiting for the arrivals.

First the cabin crew walked out, smart in their uniforms, followed by passengers. In the stream of people he spotted Gloria.

She looked different: pensive, withdrawn, lost in thought. She was casually dressed in a brown T-shirt and denims, and her long hair was tied back into a hasty ponytail. She looked jet-lagged.

He stepped forward.

"Gloria!"

When she spotted him, her face broke into a hesitant smile and they hugged each other. He took her suitcases.

"Good to see you, darling. How was your journey?"

To his surprise, she burst into tears and instinctively his arms went round her, cradling her against his chest.

"Chi-Chi wetin happen now?" He thought that using her second name would ease things up, but instead there were more tears.

He looked down at her, ignoring the looks they were getting.

Gloria dabbed at her eyes. "I'm sorry Tony. I've been such a diva lately."

Tony shook his head. "Don't worry about it. Let's just get you home."

She managed a wan smile. She put her hand into his and they walked out of arrivals.

***

The following Monday, Ada was at her desk first thing in the morning. She adjusted herself in her chair and waited for her computer to boot up. She looked up while she waited for it to load and saw Tony Okoli coming into the office with a beautiful young woman. She was tall and fair-skinned, like him. She was wearing a strappy cream dress and a wide gold belt with matching shoes, and her hair fell in brown curls to her shoulders. *The benefits of a Brazilian weave*, Ada thought to herself cattily.

Tony and the unknown visitor were smiling and deep in conversation, oblivious to everyone but themselves.

Ada was struck by a sudden wave of anger and jealousy. *What is wrong with me?* she thought. *Why am I letting this man affect me like this? I don't even know who she is. She might be a client.*

She might also be the reason why he had stopped the kiss the other night.

As he passed, he murmured a "good morning" to all the staff. Instead of answering, Ada switched her attention to the computer and started typing away furiously. Out of the corner of her eye, she could see them heading for Mrs Oseni's office.

Maybe it was his sister.

But he only had one sister.

Maybe a friend? Well, this one looked like an old friend – it was easy to see from the body language that their interaction had the casual ease of long acquaintance.

There was a sinking feeling in the pit of her stomach. His words from the night at his house flooded back to her.

"You are a wonderful person and very attractive, but my life is like a roller-coaster at the moment and the last thing you need is for someone like me to complicate yours. I cannot have a relationship with you – or anyone else."

Get real girl, she scolded herself. *Did you really think he wanted anything lasting?*

She tried to focus on her work but she couldn't. Images of his lips pressed against hers, and the quickening sound of his heartbeat when he drew her closer, kept replaying with frightening regularity.

How did I allow myself to be played like this? she

wondered. So, he had been pleasant, displayed some interest in her as an employee, been there for her after Mr Obi's attack and shown understanding. He had pushed her forward to be considered for the management training course. Those were the actions of a good employer.

But he had also charmed, flirted and kissed her. Those were the actions of an experienced player.

All you were was a pleasant diversion – a plaything while he probably waited for his dream girl to come back from wherever she'd been.

Ada pulled out a file of invoices and began to work on them, conscious that Tony and his lady-friend were still in the office behind her. She was happy for the task as it gave her a chance to concentrate on something apart from her feelings.

"This one na hot, hot love o," Olu whispered, sliding into the chair at his desk opposite her.

Ada didn't look up from her work, her fingers hovering over the keyboard in midair.

"What do you mean?" She needed to know.

"Don't you read *City People*? There was a story there about our new assistant managing director. Apparently, that babe is his childhood sweetheart. She is a lawyer, trained and works in Washington, D.C. Her father owns a large chunk of real estate in Lagos and Abuja – some kind of banker, I think. There was a picture in it of the two of them together at some function in London a couple of years ago."

"I don't read gossip magazines," Ada said dully. This was one of those few moments that she wished she did.

Olu laughed and turned his attention to his work, while Ada tried to stem the waves of disappointment and indignation lacerating the walls of her heart.

Feelings can deceive, fool and delude, she thought. *They can make you imagine a future with a man who isn't yours.*

She resolved she was never going to let feelings do this to her again.

The door to Mrs Oseni's office opened again and Ada decided she needed to make a hasty trip to the ladies', before Tony could emerge with his visitor.

***

Later that evening, Ada was at home in the communal kitchen preparing a pot of stew when Liz came back.

"We had so much food left over that I ended up with this bag full of Scotch eggs, meat pies, puff puff, chin chin and some curried chicken," she announced, holding up a bag. "The benefits of working as a catering assistant in one of the big hotels in Ikoyi."

"Sounds great," Ada said unenthusiastically and added some seasoning to the stew.

"What is wrong?"

"There is nothing wrong with me." Ada banged the pot down on the wooden table. The other women in the kitchen glanced over at her.

"Sisi Ada, wetin now?" one of them asked. "E be like say una wan use dat pot to panel beat someone's head o!"

She is a good mind reader. Ada knew whose head she felt like seriously panel-beating at this moment, but kept her thoughts to herself. She had no intention of sharing her problems with her neighbours. They thrived on gossip, just as cars relied on petrol.

Liz took one look at her face, put down her bag and went to help her with the food.

"It is well," she murmured soothingly.

Ada wasn't too sure.

Later on, when they had settled down in their room, Liz brought up the subject again.

"You are just picking at your food. What's your problem sef?"

"It's nothing," she began, but Ada could not keep up the brave face any longer and put her plate down. "It's just me. I have been so stupid."

"Is it that handsome boss of yours?"

"Am I that transparent, eh?"

"How long have I known you now? Almost five years. I think I have some idea of what gets to you. You've not been yourself lately. One minute I hear you singing and humming round the house. Now your face is like one of the people coming to sympathise with the bereaved and you're moody and irritable. I see your face when you talk about this man – it comes alive!"

"He invited me out, you know." Ada's eyes filled with

tears. "He invited me out about two weeks ago."

"You kept that to yourself."

"I didn't want to get my hopes up. And I didn't want to deal with questions I couldn't answer myself."

"So, he took you out. What happened?"

She told Liz everything that had taken place over the past few weeks.

"Then this morning, his fiancée came to the office. And, everyone seems to know that she is his fiancée – everyone except me." Ada was crying now. "Apparently news of their impending engagement is in all the lifestyle magazines and being the literary snob I am … I hadn't read them!"

Liz was quiet for some time. "It is well, Ada," she finally said. "I knew you had feelings for him, but I had no idea that things had progressed like this. At least he was honest enough to tell you the truth before things got out of control. If he was a real player the two of you would have slept together, and you would have only found out about his fiancée later. I mean – what would you have done? He is your boss. Who would you tell your story to?"

Ada nodded numbly. Liz did have a point. No-one could say that the man had taken advantage of her. He had been out of line, but, she also played a part by reciprocating his kiss. In the end, he had done the decent thing.

"Pele. As my pastor says – the best is yet to come. I know there is a man out there that will love and appreciate you. Meanwhile, just forget this Tony Okoli and move on with your life; you have no time for all this sme-sme, jare."

Ada managed a smile. Liz was right. Life was like that. You just had to move on and look to the future.

Twelve

Ada's resolve was tested a few days later.

She was alone in the photocopying room with a pile of invoices when the door opened and Tony came in. He closed the door gently behind him. She was uncomfortable when she saw him.

"Hello, Ada," he said. "I saw you headed this way and knew I had to speak to you."

She was silent, continuing with her photocopying and not looking at him.

"I was out of line two weeks ago."

She shrugged and said nothing.

He looked at her for a long time. "I'm sorry, Ada. I meant to tell you but …"

"But what?"

He sighed.

"Look, just leave me alone, abeg. I'm not going to say anything to your fiancée, if that's why you are here."

"I guess that's what I deserve, but it's not your style."

"You don't even know me – so how do you know what my style is?" She jabbed at the start button on the photocopier, wishing it was his face instead.

"I know you aren't vindictive or insecure. At least, that's what I think. You are so different from many women I know."

"And especially different from your fiancée."

"You are both unique in your own ways. Look, Ada, I messed up and I hold my hand up. I never meant to hurt you and that was why I was trying to keep you at arm's length … but there is something about you that made me keep coming back for more. You have a way of getting under a man's skin."

"So, I'm an insect now, eh? You are blaming me for your behaviour? Are you serious at all?" She had thought he was different, but she had made a big miscalculation.

"Of course not, Ada. I'm trying in my clumsy way to tell you that I'm really sorry. Gloria was always on the cards. We went our separate ways in our early twenties but as we got older we decided to give it a go, and we seemed to fit. We worked. Our parents have wanted us to get married since we were kids and it seemed the natural thing to do."

Ada raised her head so she could have a good look at his eyes. They said you could tell a person by his eyes. This guy actually sounded genuine.

"And is that what *you* want for your life?"

"I don't know," he said sadly.

"So, when we kissed – you were in your 'I don't know what I want for my life' mode, eh?"

She saw something like shame in his eyes but it was quickly replaced by a look of faint irritation. "I think you may have misread my intentions." His voice took on a matter-of-fact tone. "I'll admit it. I enjoyed talking to you and I found you attractive and for a second I lost my head, but I never, ever gave you any false promises about the future."

"You just decided to be economical with the truth about your fiancée."

"Look, Ada, I can understand that after what you have been though with Mr Obi – you probably think that all men are after the same thing."

She looked at him, her eyes challenging as if to say: *And you aren't?*

"I can't tell you how sorry I am," he said.

"There is nothing to apologise for," she said, shrugging. "I just want to draw a line through it and move on."

"I understand that." He nodded awkwardly. "Again, I never meant to hurt you, Ada. I mean that."

She turned away from him and carried on photocopying. She could feel his eyes boring into her back.

***

Tony nodded to the security guard who pressed the button to open the electric gates. Banana Island was the ultimate playground of the city's super-rich – the athletes, musicians, corporate executives, lawyers, high-ranking military and political rulers – and Gloria's family, the Onwukas.

The imposing mansion was one of many in the gated community. Its Grecian-style pillars made of marble and quartz and large French windows made it seem as if it belonged more in a plantation in the Deep South of the

United States than Nigeria. The terraced garden bloomed with African orchids, hibiscus and wild roses and beyond it were the tennis court and a large swimming pool.

He parked his car in the front of the house where it joined the collection of jeeps, a Rolls-Royce and a BMW. A white-haired steward came out to greet him.

"Good morning, Oga. Miss Gloria dey expect you."

"Good morning, Uncle John," Tony replied warmly, stretching out his hand to the older man, who bowed before accepting it. Tony hated when he did that. "How is the family?"

"Very well, sah. My eldest, Sarah, is starting secondary school soon. Chief has been so good to us."

Tony nodded and the man showed him into the house. John had been with the Onwuka family for years, but there was something about the whole idea of paying someone to wait on you that Tony found difficult to swallow. Even when he was growing up, it didn't sit well with him. It was one last vestige of colonialism and he abhorred it. He prided himself on the fact that he could cook and wash his own clothes when needed. He had someone come in twice a week to clean and do the gardening, but otherwise he did most of his chores himself.

"Big Oga and Madam are out. Can I get you a Fanta or a Coke, sah?"

"No, thank you. I'm fine."

"Let me tell Miss Gloria you don come."

"Thank you."

He showed Tony into the house and opened the door to one of the sitting rooms. Tony settled himself down into one of the chairs that faced the garden. From where he sat he could see the boats on the lagoon. Little dots on a big blue endless canvas.

Hey, he thought to himself, I can use that phrase somewhere in my book.

They were two people alone in the world. Like little dots on a big blue endless canvas.

He brought out his phone and typed the words, saving them as a note and, as he did so, he thought about the woman he had come to see.

Maybe that was what they both were. Little blue dots on a canvas already lovingly prepared for them by family long before they knew what they wanted in life. She was the girl next door, his friend and his confidante. Maybe that was why things had never progressed beyond the kissing stage. They had something really special between them and maybe they both knew what might happen if they crossed the line into intimacy.

Gloria had pledged to herself to wait till they got married and he respected her wishes. He remembered the last time he had come home on holiday. They had been in this house, in her bedroom. Her parents were out of the country and they had the house to themselves. He had kissed her but she had laughed nervously and gently pushed him away.

"I don't want to spoil things," Gloria had said. "We are

going to get married, aren't we? No need to rush."

At the time, it had not really bothered him; he had put it down to any number of things and pushed it to the back of his mind.

Then he had moved back to Nigeria and met Ada. The instant pull to her was unlike anything he had ever experienced with Gloria – or any other woman he knew.

It was like a fire threading its way through every part of his body and when he held her and felt her trembling against him he realised that Gloria had never made him feel like this. When he kissed Gloria at the airport it had been pleasant. Not bad but pedestrian. No sparks. It was like … like … he couldn't even voice it to himself. Like kissing a sister.

They had been friends since they were young.

The friendship endured although they attended different primary and secondary schools, and universities, sometimes in different countries. They stayed in contact, met up sometimes, wrote, e-mailed and Facebooked each other.

The question now was: could they be more than friends?

"Tony." He felt her presence before she called his name.

Gone was the sophisticated outfit that she'd worn to his office: the high heels and designer clothes. Her hair was tied back into a ponytail, her face had been scrubbed clean of make-up and her eyes were red. She was wearing a plain T-shirt and jeans and looked as if she had been sleeping. "Babes – what's wrong?"

Gloria stood still, she was, looking at him.

Oh boy. She has found out about Ada. He squared his shoulders, waiting for the explosion.

"Sorry I kept you waiting. I've been doing lots of thinking."

"So have I," he sighed. She sat down next to him and took his hands, and then she lifted her face to him.

"Tony … we've got to talk."

"I know."

"Tony, I love you. I always have, and part of me always will."

Her words made him feel uneasy then. This sounded too valedictory – a kind of swan song. If she knew about Ada he wished she would just come out with it.

"Gloria …"

"Hear me out, Tony. Please, let me finish. I need to say what has been on my heart for some time."

"Alright, I'm listening."

She looked away and then she turned back to him so her gaze was level with his. "I can't marry you, Tony."

He swallowed, a sense of relief mingling with guilt.

"Gloria …"

"I'm in love with someone else," she blurted out.

Tony stared at her and then he heard the door open behind them.

Tony and Gloria turned at the same time, Chief Onwuka

came into the room. His face lit up when he saw them and he hugged Tony.

"Anthony! How are you, my son?" the chief asked. Tony pulled himself together and put a bright smile on his face.

"Good afternoon, sir. I'm very well."

"I told Mama Gloria: 'I know Tony will be knocking at our door the minute Gloria is back'."

"Yes, sir." Tony surprised himself by managing to keep the smile on his face. He glanced quickly at Gloria whose eyes were imploring him to keep his mouth shut.

Does she really think I would say anything? He was still in shock.

"I will leave you young people alone," said the chief. "I'm sure you have lots of things to talk about instead of listening to an old man."

Tony knew that this was their cue to say *Oh no, Daddy, of course not*, but his head was refusing to process all the information it had churning around inside it. Gloria said something inaudible instead and the old man smiled and climbed the stairs to the next floor where his private quarters were located.

Gloria dragged Tony into the one of the smaller rooms, away from the prying eyes and ears of the house helps, and closed the door.

"Tony ..." She was breathing heavily, pacing the floor, unable to meet his eyes.

"Sit down, Gloria."

"Let me explain … I have to explain."

"Sit down. This isn't a court of law."

She sank into one of the sofas and he joined her, leaving a little distance between them.

She ran a hand over her head. "I just … I don't know where to start."

"Start anywhere you like, Gloria. Just tell me the truth."

Tears welled up in her eyes. "Emeka." She only reverted to his Igbo name when she was upset. "I've really messed up."

"Gloria …"

"Tony you don't understand. I'm pregnant."

How? Who? It was Tony's turn to run his hand over his head. *How does a girl who hardly lets you kiss her manage to fall pregnant?*

"His name is Ayo." She scanned his face intently and continued. "Ayodele Smith. He is a doctor. We met at a friend's wedding in D.C." She hesitated and shook her head. "I'm so sorry, Tony. I never meant to hurt you."

He looked at Gloria, who was staring at him. He was confused, surprised, relieved all at once.

He was silent while she went on.

"Ayo adores me and wants us to get married immediately. I asked him to be patient because I needed time to break it to my parents - and *you*, Tony."

Tony remained still, his head a scramble, and Gloria continued. She had come home for her father's 60th and wanted it to be a great occasion and not marred by this news. She knew everyone would be upset but she would tell her parents in her own time – when she was safely back on American soil.

Tony shook his head.

"Please forgive me, Tony."

"I forgive you, Gloria, but …"

"Please, Tony, help me out here. Let's just continue as normal till I leave. By the time I get to D.C. and it all comes out – everybody will feel sorry for you and I'll be the bad girl; I can live with that. I know it's a lot to ask, but I'm desperate here."

"Gloria … I'm not comfortable with this, and I hate lying to my parents."

Tony was torn between his friendship and affection towards Gloria and his love and desire for Ada. "Look, Tony, your dad is still recuperating. Do you really want to drop this bombshell on him now? It's just for a couple of weeks more. We can attend the birthday party together and after that I'll fly to Washington and be with the man I love. Tony, please do this one thing for me."

***

That evening, Ada was watching a documentary with Liz, who was grumbling all through the programme.

"Why do you think I would be interested in watching a programme about starving children?" Liz said. "Am I a journalist?"

"Do you have to be a journalist to care about starving children?"

117

"Na you know jo," Liz got up from the chair and stretched. "Change the channel to something more interesting. If I want to see starving children I can just walk down this street with my eyes open."

Ada's lips tightened as she clutched the remote control. She noticed Liz staring at something in the street outside the window.

"Ada, look outside."

"What is it now?"

"Ada, come here," Liz urged. "You won't believe who has just parked over the road."

She joined Liz at the window and was stunned to see Tony Okoli. They looked out and saw him getting out of his car. He locked the door and walked quickly across the road. Despite her annoyance Ada couldn't help noticing how the blue Ankara print shirt he was wearing emphasised the broadness of his shoulders and the muscles on his arms.

"The man fine o." Liz exclaimed. "God don butter your bread."

"What does this guy want now, eh?" Ada left the window and went to the door. "I will tell him to leave me alone. I'm not in the mood for all his nonsense."

Liz ran after her.

"Ada … don't start shouting at the man. Remember he is still your Oga. You still want a job o."

Ada marched down the passage and found Tony standing in front of the house greeting her neighbours in passable Yoruba. *Is there no end to this man's abilities?* she thought sarcastically.

"Good evening, Ada," he said. He looked at her like a little boy who was expecting a telling off.

"Gini? What do you want?"

"Ada, can we talk inside, please?"

"I don't see what we have to talk about," she said. "You made that clear the last time."

"Things have changed a little since then. That's why I want to talk to you."

She folded her arms over her chest and glared at him. "What makes you think I really want to hear anything you have to say?"

"I will stand out here until you listen to me," Tony said. He looked uncomfortable, but resolute.

"How have you got the guts to stand there and …"

A neighbour who was enjoying watching the whole exchange decided to add her advice. "Ada, listen to the man."

"She does have a point," said Tony, hopefully. Ignoring him, Ada turned to the woman.

"I hear you, ma," she said politely, but made no move to invite Tony in. "Say what you have to say here. I'm not going anywhere alone with you."

"You dis woman, take the man into your room and be hospitable – offer him something to drink – instead of standing on the street," added the landlady. "Do you want the world to hear your business?"

Someone tugged at Ada and, turning around, she saw it was Liz, who was looking at her as if she had committed a crime. She could feel the eyes of the landlady and her other neighbours drilling into her and she knew that her landlady and roommate would never forgive if her if she didn't listen to Tony.

She shrugged. "OK, follow me."

Liz smiled and announced rather loudly that she was going down the road to buy something – and that she would be some time.

Ada turned to go back into the house and Tony followed.

Opening the door, she was conscious of how small her room was. Now that he was in it, everything looked smaller. Even the guest toilet in his house was nearly the size of her room. He wiped away the sweat from his brow. She could have switched on the fan, but didn't. She took perverse pleasure in watching him suffer.

"Did you tell your fiancée that you are here?" she asked acidly. "Look, let me tell you something – I have heard stories about rich playboys who are looking for 'bush meat' to pick their teeth with after they've had their main meal and if you think that I'm that desperate you can take your money and—"

"Ada!" He spoke firmly, interrupting her speech, and then stepped forward and took her hands. "I'm sorry for what I did. I'm sorry for what I said, but I'm not sorry for feeling the way I do about you – and before you bring up Gloria again, it's over. We are both in love with other people. At least, I know I am in love with you."

In love? Ada stared at him, feeling the fight dissolving out of her. "I don't understand. I thought ..."

"Gloria was my attempt to be a dutiful son and marry someone my family approved of – an old family friend – but I didn't love her that way and I was struggling with the whole idea. But when she told me that she was in love with someone else – I felt so relieved that I could have cried. I jumped in the car and came down here as soon as I could."

She looked at him for a long time, and then suddenly snatched her hands away from his.

"So, because your girlfriend said she doesn't love you any more, you think you can just go for option B – the next best thing? Do you think I'm supposed to be grateful?"

"No, Ada ... what I want is for you to give me a chance."

Ada folded her arms across her chest, her face serious. "I like you, Tony. I really do, but ..."

"No buts ..." He moved closer to her. She stared at him, and he took her hands in his. "I'm crazy about you, Ada. I wake up thinking about the next time I'm going to see you, hear your voice. I even find excuses to go to accounts to just see if you are there."

She was silent for some time and then shook her head. "So, where do we go from here?"

"Well." He smiled slowly and inched closer. "We could kiss again – you know, carry on from where we left off."

Suddenly she felt shy. "Tony Okoli. What am I going to do with you?"

He leaned over to take her in his arms and she felt her heart beating so loudly that it was all she could hear when she felt him slowly draw close to her. His lips met hers in a long kiss. Its sweetness left her breathless and clinging to him.

Then he slowly lifted his head and looked down at her, longing etched on his face.

"Ada … I can't let you go now."

She caught her breath, her body tensed, and, unable to stop herself, tilted her head and traced little kisses down his face. She found his lips and kissed him again, softly at first, then – encouraged by his response – more urgently.

"Sweet Ada …" he whispered, pressing her body against his as they fell onto the sofa. One hand tightly around her waist, he slid the other hand up her back, pulling her closer to him, his lips hot against hers.

Then Ada's common sense, which seemed to have taken a break, began to kick in, bringing with it misgivings about what was happening. She pushed him away.

"Tony … No. I can't do this …"

He lifted his head and stared at her, his eyes narrowed. "What is the matter? I thought we were getting to know each other better."

She twisted away from him and placed her feet on the ground, which gave her a sense of calmness and strength.

"Tony …"

He wasted no time moving back to her side and kissing her neck. "Yes …"

Ada got up from the sofa and stood near the door.

Tony had a quizzical look on his face. "So, what is it?

"Please Tony, let's get to know each other better without jumping into bed first? Look…you've been good to me, friendly and a great support, but I need time. An hour ago I thought you were in love with Gloria and now–"

"So, you want me to show you that I'm serious …" Tony stood up, his arms crossed on his chest.

Ada shrugged. "Maybe. I know that I want to show you that I'm not cheap. That I feel a bit uncomfortable about having a relationship with my boss …"

Tony shook his head and drew her close. "Look, I'm crazy about you. I can't look at you without wanting to kiss you but – I respect your wish to take things slow. I want to show you that I'm serious."

She looked up into his face, searching for answers.

"Let me take you to dinner – so that we can continue this conversation. Is that a deal? Next Saturday night? I know a lovely restaurant."

She looked at him for a long time and then smiled.

Thirteen

Two days later her father rang to find out how she was.

She listened to him talk about life in the village, reminding herself that she and her brother really must do something for him. One day, she promised herself, they would build their father a nice house with a proper toilet and bathroom.

She sighed. She was the Ada – the first and only daughter – and, by tradition, her husband would be expected to play a big part in upgrading her father's property. But something in her rejected the idea of any man spending money on her family; it would be as if he was paying for her – as if she was some kind of object.

Her father was happy to hear about her trainee manager post. He was so proud of her. Then he spoiled it all by asking what she was doing about getting herself a nice husband. That was what every woman needed to be truly successful. *A nice husband.*

He told her that he needed some more money because he had given everything she had sent him to her brother, Fred. She hit the roof. She had already sent Fred some money to keep him going. Her father gave the usual excuses for him and she had to bite her tongue.

He went on. "You are too hard on your brother. You need to remember he is a man and not put him down because of your achievements. You need to be careful not to chase the right man away with your acada attitude."

The right man. What about Tony Okoli? He had her heart now and her feelings for him were so intense they sometimes frightened her, but she wasn't ready to talk to her father about him yet.

It was too soon.

She needed to be sure.

***

On Saturday evening Tony came to pick her up to take her to dinner.

He had reserved a table at Yellow Chilli in VI because, as was to be expected, Saturday night was their busiest time. Buying take-away from fast food joints like Mr Biggs and Chicken Republic was the limit of Ada's restaurant experience. So, it was nice to see Yellow Chilli, which she had read about in *Genevieve Magazine*. The restaurant was spacious with terracotta walls, plentiful green foilage and dark red couches and purple high seats. It had a soulful contemporary feel about it. The restaurant had two rooms – a small dining area that led to a larger area with a bar and the main dining space.

Music from Banky W filtered through the restaurant and the busy chatter from families, couples and some expats filled the air.

As they sat and ate in silence, Tony suddenly spoke up. "I have a business trip to Abuja in a month's time. It's a lovely place and I'm booked into the Transcorp Hilton …

I would love it if you came with me ..."

She looked at him. The music had now changed and a slow, romantic number had come on. A girl whose name she couldn't remember was singing about her lover, the song conspiring to play havoc with Ada's emotions.

"I don't know ..." She shrugged.

After the way her ex, Kanayo, had treated her, she had vowed to herself that, when she met the man she was going to marry, she wasn't going to start it off in the same way. Sex had just confused her the last time, making her stay in the relationship longer than she should have. She wasn't naïve enough to ignore the strong physical attraction between them and she knew that it wasn't going to be easy. But this was all still too new, and they still needed to get to know each other a lot more. Adding sex into the equation would be signing the executioner's warrant on what they had.

His hand covered hers. "Talk to me, Ada. I know we have serious chemistry between us. What really is the problem?"

She felt embarrassed. "I have stayed clear of relationships because I don't want jump into bed with every man I have chemistry with. What I need is someone who respects me enough to want to build a relationship first."

Silence. Gazing at Tony, she could feel the heat in his eyes as he studied her.

"I see where you are coming from ..." he finally said.

"I guess when you are starting a relationship – if you really want to evaluate what it's worth – it makes sense to take the physical side out of the equation. For now," he added pointedly.

"I'm glad you understand."

"I'm not saying it will be easy …" His eyes met hers and he sighed. "I find you very attractive."

She looked away and he took her hand in his.

"You're very different. Different is good. Maybe it wouldn't hurt to take things slowly this time. I would like the woman I marry to have principles she believes in. I respect that."

Ada couldn't believe her ears. Did she just hear him say the 'M word'? Less than a month dating and he was already talking marriage. She would be lying if she said it had not crossed her mind, but surely it was too soon?

He raised her hand to his lips and kissed it and she smiled at him.

He smiled back. "I don't intend to wait forever sha … I will wear you down."

Feeling bold, she fluttered her eyes at him. "Let's wait and see."

He placed another kiss on the back of her hand, sending featherlike sensations down her spine.

"You were saying?" he whispered.

Her smile faltered. This waiting thing was going to be even harder than she had imagined.

***

A few weeks later Tony shut down his computer after a long day. He picked up his keys and his briefcase and took the lift down to the car park on the ground floor. He saw that Ada was already waiting at one of the side entrances leading to the car park. She looked very fetching in a floral print dress but she frowned when she saw him.

Looking around, he saw that they were alone. He could see in her face that she had read his mind. She shook her head.

"You know what we agreed. I don't want anyone to see us together at work."

Teasingly, he said, "It's dark and, besides, what's one little kiss?"

She smiled reluctantly as his arms slipped round her again.

Fourteen

Ada slipped into the new dress that she had just picked up from her dressmaker. Tony had invited her to a birthday and she wanted to make an effort as she was going to meet his friends.

"Richard and Kunbi are great friends of mine. I went to school with Richard, and Kunbi is a really lovely person. I've told them a bit about you and I would love you to meet them at the surprise party that Richard is throwing for Kunbi."

Ada felt a bit pressurised. "It's all a bit scary."

"Don't worry about it. They will take one look at you and fall in love with you just as I have done."

So, she had raided her savings and bought six yards of Dutch wax from a trader on Nnamdi Azikiwe Street.

The fabric had a blue background patterned with pink flowers. The dress was off the shoulder, knee-length and tight-fitting, billowing out into fish-tail frills at the hem. Ada had seen the design in a magazine and fallen in love with it; the tailor had been able to recreate the style perfectly.

Her hair had been freshly plaited and was piled high and she had completed the outfit with gold earrings.

Tony's eyes had widened when he came to pick her up and she had let him into her room.

"I like ..." he said, grinning and pulling her to him.

"You look so beautiful."

"You look good yourself."

She had never seen him dressed like this. In a formal evening suit, a black dinner jacket over a white winged-collar shirt and black bow tie, he looked so handsome, like something out of *Ebony* magazine. He bent down to kiss her, murmuring into her ear, pulling her close and, as if he couldn't help himself, his hand rested lightly on her waist.

"It's times like this that I regret having made that stupid promise. You look absolutely …" his lips moved to her neck, " … deliciously gorgeous."

Ada was swept up by the passion in his voice and felt herself weakening. If he touched her once more, she feared that her resistance would crumble.

Then she heard his reluctant sigh. "Come on. Let's get out of here …"

She broke away to smooth her dress and caught Tony's eyes looking at her hungrily.

She smiled to break the tension and saw the serious look on Tony's face intensify.

"You are the best thing that has ever happened to me, you know."

Ada was silent, taken aback by what this man, who seemed to have the world at his feet, had just shared with her.

The best thing. He was the best thing in her life as well. Her Mr Right.

"I love you," she whispered.

He smiled, they linked hands and left the room.

***

The birthday party was held at the function room of the Golden Gate Restaurant in Ikoyi. The foyer to the main function room had been decorated with flowers and balloons and the lights were low and muted. There were about twenty people talking and enjoying refreshments.

Ada found herself being introduced to a couple of ambassadors, a pastor and his wife, a famous banker and a politician.

At first she was tongue-tied but, before long, she felt more at ease and was able to converse easily. Moving fluidly from current affairs to the arts, Tony watched her with pride.

She was sipping a pineapple drink and chatting to an up-and-coming poet when Tony and a tall dark man wearing glasses joined her.

Smiling broadly, Tony introduced Ada to the other man. "This is my friend Richard Balogun. He is a lawyer but don't hold that against him."

Richard smiled and shook her hand warmly. "Ada, I presume?"

He nodded his head approvingly at Tony.

"The birthday girl will be here soon. Kunbi's sister will be bringing her shortly – she thinks she is meeting up with some friends, going shopping and then coming here for dinner with them."

Just before Tony dragged her away to meet another friend, she saw Richard whisper something in his ear, and Tony gave a wide smile in response.

When Richard moved away, Tony took her hand.

She asked him what Richard had said, and he replied, "He said I should marry you fast before someone steals you away," Tony said.

He grinned at her, filling her heart with all kinds of possibilities. Then she heard a loud cheer and people clapping.

"The birthday girl has arrived. Let me introduce you to her."

They moved through the restaurant to meet a petite, curvy, fair-skinned woman with laughing eyes and a contented smile. Kunbi Balogun was wearing a simple dark blue skirt and blouse with gold leaves. Her smile widened when she turned in Ada's direction.

Ada didn't know why, but she felt sure that she was going to like this woman. "Happy Birthday. It is very nice to meet you."

"Let's have a chat in a moment." Kunbi squeezed her hand and turned to some other guests who were waiting.

Tony put an arm around Ada and they joined the others in the large function hall.

***

Romantic music played gently in the background as Ada glanced around the room. Guests sat enjoying their food with the birthday girl.

Tony whispered her name and Ada felt the light touch of his hand against hers. He leaned across and kissed her. At that precise moment she knew without a doubt that she loved him – and wanted to spend the rest of her life with him. Then he kissed her again, ignoring the other people at the table with them. She was glad that the lights were dim.

He lifted his head, his voice gentle, his breath fanning her cheek. "Did I embarrass you?"

Ada felt a little lost for words. *Is that the oyinbo way? Kissing in public like two teenagers?*

"You are the most beautiful woman here." His eyes met hers. "One ambassador's wife told me she was going to ask you for the number of your designer."

A few months ago she would have said he needed to have his eyes tested but she was more secure in herself now, so she smiled. "Thank you. I am flattered."

Oblivious to everyone around them, they were lost in conversation, enjoying each other's company.

Than Ada stopped eating and went silent.

"Earth to Ada …" Tony joked. "Hey … speak to me."

Ada was staring at a woman she recognised. Dressed in a tight-fitting red off-the-shoulder gown, she was talking to a well-dressed young man.

"Isn't that your sister, Samantha?"

Ada saw him stiffen as his eyes followed hers. She heard his swift intake of breath. "Of all the nights for my kid sister to be out …"

"Tony … what is the problem?"

Tony gripped her hand. "Don't worry. I will sort it out. We might be leaving soon anyway."

Ada stood her ground. "Tony – I don't understand. Sort what out? First you bring me here to meet your friends, then before we even get a chance to greet them properly – you are behaving as if you have seen a ghost."

"Ada, I will explain everything …

Ada stared at him and at that moment she heard a cold sardonic laugh coming her way. With an incredulous look on her face, Samantha appeared in front of Ada and Tony.

"Tony, what is all this?" She spoke loudly, ensuring she was audible above the music.

Tony hesitated and Ada began to feel indignant.

"Sam, will you keep your voice down?" Tony's whisper was angry.

Samantha narrowed her eyes and she squinted at Ada. "Wait. Don't I know you?"

"I don't think you do." Ada meant it. Samantha just saw her as a receptionist and she knew she was much more than that.

Samantha snapped her fingers. "That's it! I remember you. You were quite rude to me the day I came in to see Tony. I found it quite offensive, actually."

"I'm sorry if you feel that I offended you."

Samantha let her eyes travel over Ada, starting from her hair and working down to the tips of her freshly pedicured toes, peeking out of her high pink sandals.

The man Samantha was with came to join them. He looked curious.

Then he turned to Tony. "How now, Tony? Long time no hear."

Tony ignored him and addressed his sister. "Samantha, we will discuss this later. We are here to celebrate with Kunbi."

Her hands on her hips, Samantha shook her head. "Does Gloria know about this?"

Her companion put a hand on her shoulder. "Biko, Samantha, now is not the time and the place."

She pointed at Ada. "As for you … I know your kind. Always on the lookout for some rich boyfriend."

Ada pushed her chair back and stood up. "How dare you talk to me like that? You know nothing about me."

Samantha took a step towards Ada. By this time they were attracting curious glances from other guests. "I can talk to you any way I like. My brother is engaged to be married to someone I consider a sister and I'm not going to sit and watch him ruin his life."

Tony's lips twisted sardonically. "My life is messed up enough as it is. Ada is the one thing in it that makes it worthwhile. So, keep your opinions to yourself until you know all the facts - alright?"

"Dad will hit the roof ..."

"Uche," Tony said, addressing the man at Samantha's side, "Take your girlfriend out of here before I say something I regret."

Ada could not bear to hear any more. She picked up her bag and turned to leave.

"Ada!" Tony tried to stop her but she pushed past him and made her way to the door.

***

Ada stood in front of the restaurant wondering whether to take a taxi or run down the road in her long dress and catch a bus. Taxis were expensive but, right now, she didn't care. She needed to get away. Far away. She tried to forget about the imploring look Tony had given her before she left.

She had never been so insulted in her life. What gave his sister the right to talk to her like that ... but she felt uneasy and she couldn't shake it.

Then she heard Samantha's voice behind her.

"Just what do you think you are playing at with my brother?" she hissed. "He has a fiancée. He is engaged to be married and he doesn't need some money-grubbing thing like you trying to mess up his life."

Ada closed her eyes. She was tired and her head ached; her heart even more so.

"Go back inside, Samantha. This is really none of your business. It's between me and your brother."

"Well, I'm making it my business. I want you to leave him alone."

"Samantha, your brother is an adult and makes his own decisions."

"What are you on about? He is engaged to somebody else. It was announced last week at her father's 60th birthday. We were all there."

Ada stared at the younger woman. "Last week?"

"Yep." A small smile lurked around Samantha's lips. "It was a big social event. Her father welcomed Tony into the family. I've got the pictures on my phone, if you want to see them."

Ada shook her head, turning back to the road. She flagged down a passing taxi and, without negotiating the price or telling him her destination, she got in.

She bit her lip until she could taste blood. She wasn't going to cry over this man again.

She looked back and saw Tony standing there with his sister.

This taxi ride will cost me a week's earnings. I dare not think about the cost that Tony's behaviour will have on my heart.

***

When Liz came back that evening the room was in darkness, but she could see from their neighbours that they had electricity - a rarity for them. She switched on the light and saw Ada asleep in a chair next to the window.

"What's all this? Ada?"

Ada struggled awake and rubbed her eyes.

"Something dey chase you for bed? Why are you

sleeping on a chair huddled up like an old woman?"

Ada shook her head, pulled her wrapper up over her shoulders and peered out of the window. The road was quiet except for a couple of drunkards weaving along the pavement. They stopped to point at a street walker who made some rude gestures at them.

Ada turned away.

Life went on, but, in her heart, everything had come to a standstill.

"Ada. What happened?"

Ada took a deep breath and began to speak.

***

The next morning she woke up and wished she hadn't. There were no missed calls or messages on her mobile phone.

So, that was the end. The end of love. The end of deceiving herself that he was any different from the rest.

It was the weekend.

She really should have learned by now but her heart still stubbornly believed that things would work out.

Sunday came, and still no phone call. Liz went to church, leaving Ada alone with her thoughts.

Why had he lied to her? Why had he let her go through all that embarrassment with his sister? Samantha had practically accused her of being a money-grubbing runs girl … amongst other things.

Why I have been so stupid?

Fifteen

It was two o'clock on Saturday morning and Tony sat with his eyes closed, his head down and his hands folded in his lap. He heard the sound of the automatic sliding door and fresh air blew in, replacing the sharp, antiseptic smell of the waiting room.

A young woman sat down next to him.

She put an arm around him, squeezing his shoulder. "He is going to be fine. I mean it. Dad's a fighter."

"Sam ... I caused this. I was harsh."

His sister sighed and laid a hand on his shoulder. "Let me get you something to drink. Water, a coffee, a cup of tea?"

Tony closed his eyes again. "Thanks, Sam. Coffee. Black. Appreciate it."

Tony opened his eyes and watched one of the doctors with a stethoscope slung around his neck, in deep conversation with a nurse.

He remembered the accident and emergency wards he'd seen when he was in England. The typical inner-city hospital A&E department was full of people with broken limbs, cuts and bruises; drunks screaming obscenities; police officers bringing in people who had got into fights; orderlies mopping blood and vomit off the floor; and nurses running around with patients on trolleys.

But this one was a total contrast. The walls were cream

and the waiting-room seats were dark-brown leather. A big bowl of fresh flowers sat on a glass coffee table strewn with the latest copies of *Esquire*, *Ebony* and *Cosmopolitan*. There were a few patients waiting to be seen: an elderly man with anxious eyes, a pregnant woman, and a teenage boy lost in his own world with his iPod and earphones, his mouth moving wordlessly to the beat.

***

Straight after the party, Tony had driven to his parents' home in VI. He drove at breakneck speed and it was only thanks to the traffic lights that he didn't have an accident. Tony wanted to tell his parents about Ada himself, before Samantha could get to them. She beat him to it.

His parents had been shocked. His mother worried about what the Onwukas would think. His father was cold and silent, and then he started building himself up slowly into a rage. Tony was being taken for a fool; Ada was a gold-digger – Samantha had already told him about her. He would never consent to such a relationship. In fact he would disown him if he continued seeing Ada.

"So, you have left Gloria, a girl you have known since you were a child, a practising lawyer from a good home, for some Lagos girl …"

"You don't even know Ada!"

"She is a receptionist earning peanuts! All she's interested in is our money."

Tony laughed then. "Yeah. That's all that matters to you, isn't it? Our money! Your money!"

"What do you mean by that?"

"Dad, I'm an adult. I've got to live my own life. I can't let you keep making my decisions for me. I want to sort out my own life, find my own path."

Chief Okoli stopped pacing and turned to his son, jabbing his finger towards him. "We stood and watched you when you left the job of a lifetime in the city to go and follow your heart to become a writer. Now you want to follow your heart again and you expect us to give you our blessing. After everything we have done for you – you owe us more than this."

Tony was fast losing his patience. "*Owe*? All you have done for me is what a father is supposed to do for a child and one day, God willing, I will do the same for mine."

His mother shouted, hands on her hips: "Emeka! Don't talk to your father like this. Biko! Has this girl possessed your senses?"

Tony picked up his keys and marched towards the door. "Look, I can't do this right now. I've got to go."

His father's voice was getting louder. "Emeka, if you walk out of that door ..."

Tony spun around, "what will you do, Dad? Take the company from me? Take the house, the car and all the other things you have given me, instead of just listening to me for once and finding out what I'm about, what I want out of life?"

Chief Okoli looked stunned. The muscles worked in his neck as he growled. "Get out! Get out of my house. You … you ingrate!"

Tony stormed out of the house, slamming the door behind him, ignoring his mother's pleas.

He hadn't yet put the key in the ignition when he heard his phone ringing; he glanced at it and saw it was his mother. He ignored it and drove out of the compound at top speed. He kept driving and then the phone rang again. Long incessant plaintive bleats, like a baby crying to be noticed, but still he did not pick it up.

When he got home, he saw that he had several text and voice messages. The first one made his blood run cold. It was from Samantha.

Dad has been taken to Reddington Hospital. He collapsed soon after you left. Please call me. Sam.

***

Mrs Okoli looked up when her son approached her and sighed heavily. "The doctors have been in with him since we arrived."

A nurse beckoned and they went into the hospital room. Chief Okoli lay sleeping. Tony was shocked at how small and vulnerable he looked. He was such a powerful man, it was hard to see him so helpless and weak, attached to tubes. The room was silent except for the faint hum of the air conditioner and the technology that was keeping his father alive.

Tony leaned over him and his father's eyes flickered.

"Emeka. You are here?"

"Of course, Dad. I came as soon as Mum told me."

Samantha hovered in the background and a nurse came in and checked Chief Okoli's pulse. Tony stared down at his hands, twisting them as if by doing so he could expel the turmoil within him.

He saw his father open his bloodshot eyes and his lips curve into a slight smile.

"I'm still here. Not going anywhere. I need to keep an eye on you people."

Tony shook his head. "Dad ... I'm so sorry ... for what I said ..."

His father closed his eyes. "Emeka ... It's OK. It's OK. Where is your mother?"

Tony's mother came up to the bed and took her husband's hands.

"I'm here, my husband."

He saw the relief in his father's eyes and the look of tenderness that passed between them. He almost felt jealous of the love they had.

***

Mrs Okoli, Tony and Samantha went back to the family home. Tony felt a sudden need to be around his family at a time like this and was going to stay in the guest room.

"I haven't spent a night alone in 31 years, except for the times when Chief used to go on business trips," his mother said, sighing.

They spoke late into the night about happier times until Samantha went to bed, leaving Tony and his mother to reminisce.

"Emeka, talk to me. What is going on?"

He sighed deeply and then told her about Gloria and the baby.

He could see her horrified expression.

"I knew this was going to be upsetting to you. It's one of the reasons why I felt it best not to say anything. Gloria on the other hand has her own reasons – ones you can deduce yourselves."

"What kind of nonsense is all this? I don't know what is worse – her behaviour or you carrying on with a receptionist!"

"Mum, it's not like that."

"So, how is it then?"

"We were both kids when we started dating. We probably had these stupid ideas about making our parents happy. At one point we went our separate ways. We got back together again but we were just going through the motions. At last, we realised that we couldn't keep pretending to each other any more."

His mother shook her head.

They sat in silence, both lost in their thoughts, as the night stretched before them.

Sixteen

Ada dragged herself out of bed on Monday morning. It had been a horrible weekend. A weekend alternating between recriminations and wanting to call Tony and waiting for him to call.

It was a relief to be at her desk in accounts. She could immerse herself in formulae and spreadsheets and shut off all the stuff going on in her head.

She felt a pair of eyes on her. She turned round and found Olu.

"What is it now, Olu?"

His eyes were cold and a mocking smile played around his lips. "It might be something and it might not be anything. It depends on how you look at it, I suppose. This life never fails to amaze me sha."

"You are talking in riddles now and I have no time. I've got to get this report done before the end of the day."

"No shaking. With your connections in this place – no Oga can hassle you."

Ada looked up. "What do you mean by that?"

"Hmm. Ada, you are friends with the powerful people – the Ogas at the top, the Alayes, the Ogbuefis. I am just small fry to you now o."

Ada stared at him and couldn't help noticing that other colleagues were also casting pointed looks at her.

Wetin happen? She stared at them, puzzled at the

change of atmosphere. Instead of the usual playful banter and good-natured jokes, she felt their scorn.

"What is going on with everyone this morning?"

As the words left her mouth she heard the sound of an e-mail landing in her inbox. She looked on her screen.

It was from Mrs Oseni, the head of department. Ada's boss, Mrs Solanke, had been copied in.

Ada. Could I see you in my office?

What had she done? Had there been an error with the figures she had submitted that had resulted in the company losing millions?

Silently, she walked through the office, noticing the cold stares from her colleagues until she reached Mrs Oseni's door.

She knocked and was asked to come in, which she did, carefully closing the door behind her. Mrs Solanke was there as well, looking at her with an expression she couldn't read.

Mrs Oseni spoke quietly. "Please have a seat."

Ada sat gingerly, while Mrs Oseni carried on typing on her computer.

Ada instinctively knew that something was horribly wrong. She felt as if she needed to open the windows to get air to breathe.

"Ada, you are a valued member of this department. Your colleagues and managers have nothing but good things to say about you …"

Ada waited for the punchline. *But* …

"But some very serious information has come to light and we have decided to speak to you about it, before management step in."

Ada sat up straighter. "Management? Sorry, I don't understand what all this is about."

Mrs Solanke handed her a piece of paper. "Ada, I think you need to read this e-mail. It has been circulating all round the office. Apparently Mr Obi e-mailed it to the M.D. and copied the board members and HR."

Slowly, as if she was in a trance, Ada took it and read, her heart tightening in her chest.

```
From: Ignatius Obi <ignatiusobi@hotmail.
com>
Date: Friday, 20 November 2009 8.40
To: DeptHeads <deptheads@cityfinance.com>
cc: Board Members <boardmemberscityfin-
ance.com>
Subject: Ada Okafor


Dear Sir

I want to bring the matter of my unfair
dismissal to your esteemed notice.

You will recall that I have worked
tirelessly and with dedication for this
company for close to eleven years. I feel
that I have been sacked without proper
redress. This is all because of a current
employee of yours - Miss Ada Okafor.
```

I would like to state that the aforementioned Ada Okafor and I were lovers for several months before the arrival of your son from England. I am not proud of my actions in having a relationship out of wedlock but it is as Shakespeare said - To err is human. One evening after work we arranged to meet up and were we were about to engage in our usual amorous activity, but your son walked in on us and she started screaming that I was attacking her. If what he saw was an attack, ask me how I know about the L-shaped birthmark just above her heart.

That day I protested and told Mr Okoli junior that she was my girlfriend and we had been keeping it secret because of company policy. Agatha Nneli can testify to this because they both work on reception and this was discussed during their usual woman-to-woman talks. Seeing us together Mr Okoli was furious and pushed me out of the room, whereupon I was then seriously assaulted by security before being pushed out onto the public street like a common criminal. I ask you, Sir - is this the way I, myself Ignatius Chukwudi Obi, should be treated after all the years of service (ten years and seven months exactly) I have given from the sweat of my brow to your company?

Since I was sacked by your company for gross misconduct I have been unable to get another job and have had to resort to relying on relatives and well-wishers to even put food on the table for myself and my family.

In a company that prides itself on its fairness and open policy, I fear that nepotism is slowly rearing its head. A girl that was working as an accounts clerk/receptionist is put forward for a management role because she is having a relationship with the Assistant M.D.

I have consulted with my lawyers, Zenith Partners, and they will be contacting you in due course as I intend to take this matter to the highest court in the land, in order to prove my innocence and restore my professional, ethical and moral standing. The press will also be interested in hearing how company operates its promotion policy and how it treats its workers.

Yours sincerely

I C Obi (Esquire)

Ada shook her head slowly. "Is this some kind of a bad joke? Somebody playing an April Fool's prank long after the date? This is all fabricated! I swear it's a lie."

Mrs Oseni folded her arms across her chest. "So are you categorically stating that you and Mr Okoli are not in a relationship?"

"That's not what this is about. I am being accused of using my body to get ahead in this firm and it is not true.

I never had a relationship with Mr Obi. He attacked me and Mr Okoli stopped him from …" Her voice trailed off.

"So, is this when you began the relationship?" Mrs Solanke said, adjusting her glasses.

Ada shook her head. "No. I mean it wasn't till a couple of months after that."

"And when we offered you the trainee position were you or were you not in a relationship with Mr Okoli?" Mrs Solanke pressed on.

"No, I wasn't."

Mrs Oseni unfolded her arms. "So, it was after you got the trainee position that he asked you to go out with him?"

Ada closed her eyes and remained silent. It was like they were twisting everything.

Mrs Oseni continued. "Even the hint of scandal from a member of my staff cannot be tolerated."

Ada shook her head. "I would never do anything to bring this department into disrepute."

Chineke Father God, what is all this nonsense. Floor, open up and swallow me. Please tell me this is not happening. The man is talking about suing the company for wrongful dismissal. Going to the press…

"You still haven't answered my question. Are you having an affair with the assistant managing director?"

Ada looked up. "We are not having an affair. Yes, we are going out but …"

She saw Mrs Oseni and Mrs Solanke exchange

knowing glances and knew that things were going to get a lot worse before they got any better.

***

When she left Mrs Oseni's office, she saw that her colleagues were still in huddles murmuring. When they saw her approach they started going back to their desks.

Mrs Oseni wasn't impressed. "Could we get some work done here, please? Less talk and more work." She went back inside and then slammed the door.

Ada sank into her chair and tried to shut out the inquisitive looks and the persistent murmurs. She caught Olu's glare and turned back to the computer.

She had to speak to Tony. Had to explain ...

She heard her phone vibrate, telling her she had received a text.

It was Tony.

Ada. Please call me when you have a moment.
Tony.

She didn't want to phone him. She needed to see his face. Look into his eyes. Hear him speak into the confusion of her mind – listen to his explanation about Samantha while he listened to hers about this stupid letter.

She got up, dazed, and walked towards the lifts. She was about to press the button to call the lift when she heard someone call her name.

It was Agatha. Her face was hard and her lips curled

in scorn.

"Na wa o." The sarcasm hung heavy in the air. "Your secret has caught up with you today, eh?"

"Agatha ... get your facts right before you judge me."

Agatha stood in front of Ada, her hands on her hips, hissing in a furious whisper, "We used to be friends, we used to gist and talk and now you just ignore me and walk around with your head in the air because you are now moving with big people."

Ada was shocked at the pent-up venom that was being unleashed. "Agatha ... why are you saying all this? We've worked together for almost two years. I thought you knew me better than that?"

"I no know anybody o. Especially when position is involved. People fit change – just like that."

"If that is what you want to believe—"

Agatha hissed. "Remember Mr Obi? Did I ever tell you that he is my townsman?"

Ada frowned.

"He told me how you cost him his job. When no-one would listen to him he had to write this letter to clear his name."

"The man is lying!"

"You are the liar! Agatha this and Agatha that but all the while you are sneaking upstairs to M.D. junior because of promotion."

"It wasn't like that. I was chosen by my boss, not the assistant M.D."

Agatha laughed. "Your secret is out. I saw you and him kissing. I stayed late that evening to cover reception because there was a meeting. I saw you head for the car park and I followed you. I saw the assistant M.D. arrive and kiss you before you got into his car. You even sat in the owner's corner. Do I look like a mumu to you? I asked you months before what was going on and you told me some story about a book he gave you to read. I know the name they give women like you."

Ada felt exhausted. She shook her head, entered the lift and pressed the button to the fourth floor, saying, "You've got it all wrong," as the lift door closed.

"You see trouble dey sleep and na you go wake am. You think say you can play this game but you are just a small girl," Agatha shouted after her.

Seventeen

A couple of hours before, Tony Okoli had been on the phone to a client when his executive assistant, Mrs Sawyer, a grey-haired woman wearing glasses, came in. Elegant and middle-aged, she had an air of quiet efficiency and professionalism.

She handed him a pile of letters and gave him a hesitant look.

He finished his conversation and started casually going through them. Then he saw a brown envelope marked:

NO LONGER PRIVATE & CONFIDENTIAL

"Is this some kind of a joke?" He stared at the envelope, a quizzical look on his face. It wasn't corporate and the lettering on the address was uneven.

Mrs Sawyer looked perplexed.

Tony tore it open and began to read it. When he had finished he didn't look up.

"Mrs Sawyer, I will be with you in a few minutes. I need to make some phone calls."

She nodded and left the room, quietly closing the door behind her.

Fury descended upon him like a hot cloud. The whole idea that Mr Obi knew these intimate details about Ada filled him with a jealousy that he had never felt before.

Every word in the letter was branded into his

consciousness like hot lead melting into his soul.

L-shaped mark above her heart.

What on earth was all that about?

How on earth would he know about that unless he had seen her, touched her – made love to her? The idea made him feel physically sick.

Then his logical side began to kick in. Mr Obi had torn Ada's blouse, so he could have noticed the L-shaped mark then.

He knew Ada. She wasn't the type to be duplicitous. It just wasn't in her nature.

He wouldn't ask her. The whole thing was a mess, a big fat mess that had grown out of all proportion and could drag the reputation of the whole company into the mud if it went to court.

Surely that should be worrying him more than the image of Ada lying in Mr Obi's arms.

The man was a liar. He had seen what taken place. It was a clear case of attempted rape and the girl had been genuinely frightened. Mr Obi was just trying to drum up conspiracy theories and should not be taken seriously.

He shook his head and at that moment let go of any doubts about the woman he loved. He picked up his phone and sent Ada a text asking her to come up to see him. He wanted to reassure her that he would sort everything out, that he did not believe a word of the gossip and that things would blow over. He also needed to talk to her about what had happened at Richard and Kunbi's party and put her mind to rest.

He decided that he would call Richard for some legal advice. Just as he was about to dial, the phone rang. It was a member of the board, one of his father's right-hand men.

"Tony, what is all this nonsense in this letter? Is there any truth in it?"

Tony took a deep breath, "None whatsoever." He tried to calm the man down. "It's all lies, sir ..."

The man sighed. "People believe lies, shareholders believe lies, our competitors believe lies, and the media believe lies. If this guy decides to go to court – the company's reputation could be ruined. We can't afford a scandal, just as we are trying to rebuild the company." He shook his head. "Sorry, son. This girl may not be all she seems. Promoting her so quickly was not a good idea and to have a relationship with her – even more foolish. Always let your head rule your heart. One rule that has helped me over the past 30 years: never mix business with pleasure."

Tony heard his mobile phones ring and saw that his mother and sister were calling him at the same time.

He closed his eyes.

***

She was alone in the lift, much to her relief. She was in no mood to see or talk to anyone.

When it stopped on the fourth floor she got out and walked as fast as she could towards Tony's office.

Suddenly a group of the directors spilled out from one of the meeting rooms and stared at her.

Her heart sank, but she walked past them with her head high to Tony's office. She opened the door and went inside.

Mrs Sawyer gave her a warm smile and gestured to the plush brown sofa in the reception area.

"Mr Okoli is with his sister at the moment. If you don't mind waiting I will let him know that you are here."

Ada sank into the sofa, the realisation sinking in that this nightmare was far from over.

Mr Obi had lit the fire, Agatha had poured petrol on it and now Samantha Okoli was here in person to fan the flames. *What kain wahala is this?*

She sat down and waited. She picked up a magazine and flicked through the glossy pages without registering anything. The minutes ticked by and then the door opened slightly and she caught part of the conversation. Samantha's whiny American voice was saying, "She is a bush girl. She isn't up to our standard. You know deep down that she is only with you for the money! Open your eyes and see what's in front of you … how does this man know about all these intimate details about this woman?"

Ada listened, her heart racing. There was silence. No response from the man she loved. She caught the embarrassment in Mrs Sawyer's eyes.

Then she heard his voice. He spoke slowly. "I don't know … OK, it doesn't look good, I admit it. Don't forget, he tore her clothes so he could have seen the L-shaped mark."

Ada stood up and walked towards the door. She heard someone calling her but it was too late. She ran blindly out of the office, almost colliding with some members of staff on her way to the waiting lift.

There was no love left to fight for. She already felt the cold chill of being an outsider. The Okolis were shutting the doors against her.

She walked through reception in a daze until she found herself standing on the busy street and a woman carrying a bale of clothes on her head bumped into her.

A car screeched to a halt and the driver stuck his head out of the window, swearing at her.

Se Ore e pe? Is your head correct?

She stared back at him blankly.

***

She made it home, lay on her bed and cried so much that the landlady knocked on her door and asked her what was wrong. She replied that she had received some bad news regarding her job – which was partly true. There was no way she could ever imagine herself working for City Finance any more. Especially now that she knew what Tony really felt about her. She couldn't bear to see Tony looking at her scornfully like her colleagues because of Mr Obi's lies.

Liz came back after work to find Ada still lying on

the bed crying. Through all the sobs and wailing, she managed to work out what Ada was saying.

"Ada, listen to me, everything will be OK even though it doesn't look good at the moment. Tony is an idiot, a fool, who doesn't know a good thing when it is staring him in the face. You'll see, he will come crawling back."

Liz was alarmed to see that Ada had already packed all her stuff into a couple of suitcases.

"So, Ada, you came home, threw yourself down and cried your eyes out. Then you decided to get up and pack your things, and then threw yourself back onto the bed? What are you playing at?"

"I need to get away from Lagos immediately."

Liz looked at the friend she had known for several years. Her eyes were dull and red-rimmed. "Where will you go … what will you do? Eh, Ada, you and your stubborn pride – why not stay and defend yourself against these accusations?"

"Liz, I would have stayed. I could have stayed through all the gossip at work but, when he did not come to my defence against his sister's accusations, something died in me. I knew that I didn't want to be with a man who doesn't trust me."

"He loves you. I've seen the way this man looks at you when he brings you home."

"He hasn't got what he wants from me. That's why he keeps pursuing. That is why I need to get out of here before he starts banging down the door and demanding to see me. Now I know the truth, it is all the more difficult."

"At least tell me where you are going so I can ..."

"Can what? Tell him where I am? Why? I am like a fever in that man's blood. Once he has got what he wants from me – he will go back to those rich girls. The ones his family will approve of."

"But you cannot go ... what about the job – the traineeship – next year will be your final year of studying?"

"I will try and get another job back in the east. Port Harcourt maybe or Enugu. Or even Calabar. I am sure I'll be able to transfer my credits to another uni."

"You seem to have it all worked out. Don't tell me you are going tonight?"

"Yes. There is a night bus."

"Na wa for you. Make una think this through well well o."

Ada shrugged. She knew Liz was upset and she understood that – where would the girl find someone to share with at such short notice? But this was one of those times when she had to take care of herself.

Wiping the tears from her eyes, she sighed and picked up her suitcases. Without another glance she walked out of 25 Akinsanmi Street and on with her new life. Liz helped her with her bags to the street where she would get a bus headed for Oyingbo Garage and from there catch a bus back to the east.

***

The next afternoon Tony sat in his car staring at Ada's house. Everything looked the same. The old lady was still on the veranda, frying yam. The young men were gathered in the front yard, playing cards and ogling a group of teenage girls who walked past. The little shop that sold soft drinks was open, and a few customers stood waiting to be served.

Tony waited until evening, hoping he would see Ada, but she didn't appear. He was relieved when he saw her roommate return, though. He waited for her to greet the old woman and let herself into the house and then he got out of his car and crossed the road.

He bent his head and greeted the old woman in Yoruba.

"*E kurole ma.* Good evening, ma."

"Good evening." The old woman nodded. "*Ko sin bi mo.* She isn't here."

He knew enough Yoruba to understand what she was saying, and nodded.

He went into the house and walked to the door of the girls' room. It opened in response to his knock and Liz stuck her head out.

"Gini? What do you want?"

He tried to smile. "Don't be like that, Liz. At least hear me out ..."

She stared at him. "If you came to see her you are at least a day late."

"What do you mean? Is she OK?"

"She is fine. Well, as fine as she could be in the

161

circumstances after the way you and your family treated her."

"That's what I wanted to see her about. I don't understand what is going on, but surely she should know that I'm prepared to give her the benefit of the doubt."

Liz shrugged. "Una do well, eh … you and your family. But I'm the wrong person to talk to."

"I've been in the hospital with my father. He was in a serious condition – in fact, he still is. It was difficult to get away. I've been texting Ada all night and there has been no response. Her phone has been switched off."

"So?" Liz folded her arms over her chest.

"So, what is going on?"

"As you can see she isn't here."

"Liz, I'm tired and have had a horrible few days. Where is she?"

"Right now. Probably in the east somewhere."

His frowned. "What do you mean in the east somewhere? Don't you have a forwarding address for her?"

"No – and, even if I did, I would not give it to you."

He sighed. "Look Liz, I understand that you're protective of your friend, but if you really care about her you would want us to sort things out. I have deep feelings for Ada. I realise now that I've messed up big time and all I want to do is to see her and apologise."

"I'm telling you the truth – when Ada left here she was absolutely heartbroken. She went back home to see her father and will be there for a week or so before she decides what she is going to do next."

"What do you mean – what she is going to do next? Isn't she coming back to Lagos for her final year?

"No. She is going to take her credits to another uni."

His face fell when she said this. He did not look himself and he knew this. He looked unshaven and wore scruffy jeans and a shirt that had not seen an iron. He knew he had lost weight with all that was happening.

It serves me right. I had something good and I let it go.

"She did leave something for you, though … she said you might turn up soon." Liz went back into the room and came out with a couple of books, which she handed over to him.

"What is this?"

"The books you lent her."

Tony scratched his head and stared at the copies of *The Faminished Road* and *No Longer at Ease*. "Liz … in the name of God, give me any information you have on where she can be reached. I love her."

His eyes were laced with tears. It felt like his world was crashing down on him. He stood at the door motionless for a while.

Just when I thought I had found my perfect soulmate, I can't even hold on to her. What is wrong with me?

"Sorry. I cannot help you. Goodbye." She put her hand on the door handle.

Tony walked to the front door in a daze.

Eighteen

London, February 2014

A woman emerged from Liverpool Street station and joined the sea of people spilling out onto the pavement. Her hair had been straightened and fell sleekly to her shoulders. She was wearing a grey beret and coat and was carrying a briefcase.

The sharp air of the winter morning made workers walk briskly, like robots. They didn't spare a glance for the tourists trying to take pictures of the many statues and historic buildings around the area.

Then slowly it started. Little drops of rain building up momentum. She increased her pace and was just about to cross to the other side of the road when she heard someone call her name.

She spun round in surprise and stared at the man who had greeted her.

"I knew it was you," he said, holding out his hand. "It's Ada, isn't it? We met at my wife's party some years ago."

At first she stared at him and then her memory kicked in. "Hello," Ada said, guardedly. Richard Balogun, Tony's lawyer friend, looked older than the last time she had met him. His hair had now totally receded. He was holding a little boy of around six by the hand and looking at her curiously.

"Interesting meeting you here."

"I work just across the road." She gestured vaguely ahead.

"Where?"

"PricewaterhouseCoopers."

The man looked impressed. "It's good to see you."

"Thank you. How is your family?"

"We are all doing well."

She was silent, torn between wanting to be polite, resisting the temptation to look at her watch, yet wanting to hear more about Tony.

"I'm here on holiday. This is my son." He pointed to the young boy with him.

Ada relaxed a little. He was so cute, swinging his Hamleys toy shop bag from side to side.

She smiled at the child. "I see you've been shopping."

The boy nodded and clung to his father's hand.

Richard stood watching her. "It is a shame things didn't work out between you two."

Ada said nothing.

"Why did you just disappear like that? He almost went crazy trying to find you."

Ada shrugged. "Relationships break up. We were young." *Young enough to be deceived, young enough to listen to lies, young enough to have a heart to break, young and weak enough to capitulate to family pressure to conform.*

"I've known Tony since we were kids and never seen him that smitten. Even with his ex. He has been looking for you ever since but no-one knew where you were. Someone said you were in the east and another said you were in the States. He tried the internet and I think he even got a private detective to search for you once – still came up with nothing."

"You know how it is. We just lost touch."

Then she did look at her watch. "I really must dash now." She didn't want to hear all this. Her life was well ordered into little compartments. There was work, friends and her career. That was all she needed.

Richard looked apologetic. "Of course, of course. Sorry for keeping you – I know how things are over here."

"Yes."

"Tony actually lives in England now. He left the company soon after you disappeared. When his father got better, there was a big row so he came back here. His father retired soon after for health reasons and sister Sam heads the company now."

Sam always gets what she wants. Ada's patience was beginning to wear thin and all she wanted to do was to disappear.

Richard went on. "Tony still works as an accountant but has bigger plans. You know him ... his literary leanings. He studied part-time for an MA in creative writing and pieced together his book, all the while working full-time. By the way, he is having a book launch soon.

Ada did not understand why her heart was racing so fast as she took in some of the information that was coming at her. Tony. Left the company. Living in England. He was here. She could have bumped into him on the Tube any time.

She shrugged. "I don't have time for all that stuff any more. My job keeps me really busy. I can't remember the last time I read a novel."

Richard rummaged in his coat pocket and gave her a flyer. "It's for the book launch. It's going to be at Waterstones in Finchley on Saturday the 22nd. It would be really good if you could come."

"I'll be working that day. You know how it is. Work."

The man nodded. "I understand, perfectly."

She put the flyer into her pocket and said goodbye.

He nodded. She walked off in the opposite direction without a backwards glance.

It wasn't until she stood looking at herself in the mirror in the office toilet that she realised that her face was wet, not from the rain, but from her tears.

***

That evening Richard's words kept coming back to her, but she shrugged them off.

Ada tried to put the incident in context and calm herself down. Maybe it was a coincidence. It didn't mean anything. Tony was in her past now.

Tony. In the UK. So close, but oh so far.

It wasn't only the years that separated them. It was the pain of mistrust and betrayal. Oh well. It had taken her years to forgive herself for her youthful stupidity. Life had to go on.

Five years ago she had been a heartbroken young woman who had left everything she knew behind to start a new life in Port Harcourt. She had started at the bottom as an accounts clerk at PwC, which helped pay for her rent and her tuition fees at the University of Port Harcourt. Soon, her dedication and professionalism had got her noticed by management and someone mentioned the work placement programme being run by their parent company in London. She applied for it and completed the exam. It had been a dream come true when she was selected for the five-year work placement opportunity.

So now she wanted nothing to do with the Okoli family. Everything was about them, their name, their money, their prestige, their standing in society. Here, in London, she was her own person. She had her flat, she had her car, and she had her own job. She didn't need them. She didn't need anybody.

***

A few days after bumping into Richard, Ada found herself googling Tony's name.

Tony Okoli. Accountant Okoli has had several of his articles published in The Times, Africa Writers and recently, the New York Times. A fresh new voice from Africa, he is a writer to look out for. His first novel "Dawning of an African Son" is due for publication by Collins and Baker this winter.

Good for him, but she had moved on.

Come on girl, aren't you a little bit impressed by what Tony has done? His dreams and aspirations had come true. He was now a published author doing what he always wanted to do: write.

OK. So she was impressed but he had hurt her deeply. Even though she had recovered, she wasn't going to let him or anyone else do that to her again. Besides, she had adjusted to being single now. It was less stressful than having a man in her life.

***

A week had passed since she bumped into Richard. Life had gone on as usual. There were meetings, deadlines and work to be done. There were even times when it felt so normal that Ada had to remind herself that her meeting with Richard hadn't just been in her imagination. It had actually happened.

She swiped her card at reception and took the lift to her floor. She walked into the office and sat at her desk trying to breathe normally and force herself to smile and join in with the usual noisy office banter.

She sat and stared out of the window for a minute, trying to compose her thoughts and get her mind ready for the day. The office overlooked the heart of the City. From her desk she could make out the large imposing stone façade of the Bank of England. She shared an office with four other people. Two dizzy girls in their early twenties who seemed to have just discovered men, and a married woman who was in her forties. She was the calm sensible one who kept everyone in check and listened to their relationship problems, offering a sympathetic ear and the occasional cup of tea.

She was about to switch on the computer when she noticed a package on her desk. She opened it absent-mindedly, expecting it to be some financial report or the management accounts she was awaiting. But it was a book.

A glossy copy of a book titled *Dawning of an African Son*.

The cover had a dark blue background of the sun setting against the midnight sky. She turned to the back cover, and saw Tony Okoli staring out at her, a playful smile on his face:

Dawning of an African Son

Chidi, the son of an industrialist, and Amaka, the daughter of their cook, fell madly in love in 1970s Lagos. They embarked on a secret romance that destroyed the friendship he had with his best friend Nkem.

Nkem, frustrated at losing his chance with Amaka, spreads a lie which throws their two families into a headlong collision that ultimately tests their friendship, loyalty and everything they hold dear.

A feud that death doesn't wipe out.

A love that time cannot erase.

In his quest to be the perfect son, will Chidi chart his

own life course or conform to society's expectations and be the dutiful son?

Thirty years later they meet again at a funeral. Chidi is a top surgeon and Amaka a headmistress. One never married and the other widowed with children – will they be able to move beyond the pain of the past and find a future together?

Dawning of an African Son is an unflinching look at how class, society and identity shape the lives and destinies of three friends.

Tony Okoli is a new voice in African writing who brings a new perspective and vibrancy to African writing.

A compelling read from a master storyteller.

Ada picked it up and flicked through the pages, feeling numb. Her head was spinning. There was a small note with Tony's signature at the end.

Dear Ada,

A couple of days ago I got a call from Richard – who told me he had seen you in London. He also told me where you work, which is how I managed to send this parcel to your office.

Ada – I have been looking for you for the past five years so to find out that you are in the UK gives me a bittersweet feeling. Bitter because you were close and I didn't know but sweet because at

least I know you are doing well and – according
to Richard – looking it too.

You were a great encouragement with my writing
efforts, with all our conversations about books.
I will never forget that. I want to send this
token your way as a peace offering. I hope that
somehow you will read my heart through its pages
and realise that, for me, it was you, is you and will
always be you.

I enclose with this an invite to the book launch at
Waterstones, O2 Centre, Finchley Road NW3. It's
on the 22nd Feb. I would consider it an honour if
you were able to attend. It would be so wonderful
to see you again.

Yours

Tony

***

Ada started reading the book on the Tube. Soon she was so engrossed that she almost missed her stop.

She got home and, after making herself a cup of tea and some toast, she continued with the book, eager to know what happened in the end. Tony was a great storyteller. *Dawning of an African Son* was quite autobiographical, and part of her was scared to go on, because the book projected into the future and showed how Tony's life might be if he didn't make some hard decisions. Maybe he didn't want to end up like the protagonist, Chidi: in his mid-fifties racked with regrets and longings. The man that seemed to have let everyone else dictate his life.

Amaka stared at him.

"What do you want from me?" Her eyes were full of tears.

Something broke in him and he pulled her to him. There was no need for words or recrimination. She struggled, hitting him with her fists, calling him all the names she could remember. He held her against him until all the fight left her and she was calm again.

"I'm tired of running. All that I ever wanted is here. With you."

"What about the children?"

"Amaka, you need to wean them off you. I need you now. This is about us… They have their own lives. One is at university, the other is ready to get married. When will you have time for your own life?"

She was still shaking as his lips met hers in a long kiss. Then she opened her eyes and he traced his fingers across her face, wiping her tears away. He marvelled at her beauty – in her early fifties her face was unlined – and to him she was the same girl he had fallen in love with over thirty years ago.

"Biko … I am a mother. A mother of two big children. Look at us behaving like the teenagers we were years ago."

He nodded. He needed no reminding that she was indeed the mother of those grown children. The ones that didn't want him to see her again. The children that thought he had ruined her marriage. The boy and the girl with Nkem's eyes that looked upon him with such hatred every time he came to the house.

"Amaka," he whispered, "Just for once in our lives ... let us think about ourselves. Marry me."

She nodded and their hands interwined her hands with his.

He squeezed her hand. "We will talk to the children again. I will beg them if necessary ..."

More than thirty years after falling in love with her when she was a student at Regan Memorial Baptist School, Yaba, he finally made her his wife. It was a simple ceremony. A few friends and family. Nothing more. Despite all he had achieved, Amaka had always been the one person who held his peace, his joy and stability in her hands. As he held her close, he knew that he wanted to spend the rest of his life making up for the pain he had caused her, and, with hearts pounding, they took their first kiss as man and wife. They had been spiritual nomads. Each on their own journeys that had taken them off in opposite circles until now – the circle was complete.

Ada closed her eyes and took a deep breath. Was this what he wanted – a passionate reunion after the tears and recriminations?

The question was – what did she want?

Despite herself, she turned the page …

They lay quietly against each other, listening to each other's heartbeats, their minds dwelling on the events of the years that separated them.

Chidi looked outside and realised that faint blue arrows of day had begun to poke their fingers through the indigo sky and he smiled, knowing that this was the beginning of his own new dawn.

Amaka was the first to speak. "Why did it take you this long to come and find me – you old man?"

He chuckled slowly. "After all that … you call me an old man?" He held her close and kissed her again.

"I wanted it to be you. All the time with him – I couldn't stop thinking about you."

He put a finger on her lips. "Let's not talk about him. Not tonight … not tomorrow. Let's just try and look to our future."

She closed her eyes and smiled …

Ada closed the book. She, unlike Amaka, was not smiling.

Chidi had made some mistakes. Although Chidi had left Amaka at the mercy of a man she didn't love, she had never stopped loving him.

Just as she knew she had never stopped loving Tony.

Sometimes she would sit on the Tube on the way to work and see laughing couples in love and families with little children. Then she would wonder what life might have been like if things had turned out differently for her and Tony.

She didn't want to wake up one day old and grey, still wondering what might have been. She knew what she had to do.

Nineteen

Ada looked at herself in the mirror.

This evening she had an important event to attend.

She had decided to wear a business suit – a grey jacket and trouser suit over a turquoise silk blouse with high black shoes. Dainty turquoise earrings completed her outfit. Her hair had been straightened and fell to her shoulders in a sleek bob.

She had to be prepared. She had to know what to say and how to say it. Her whole life might change afterwards. She had rehearsed her speech over and over till she knew it in her sleep.

She took one last look at herself in the mirror, locked her flat and caught the Underground to Finchley in north London.

Around her the crowd pushed and jostled, but she was oblivious to her uncomfortable surroundings.

***

When she arrived at Waterstones, many people were already seated and others were milling around chatting.

The event organiser – a smallish woman with a clipboard – came up to her and wanted to usher her to a seat in front but she declined and went to sit at the very back. She preferred to be less visible.

From where she sat she could see the whole room. It was well lit and filled wall to wall with books. Someone had given the place their idea of an African feel with carefully positioned potted palm plants, drums and a huge map of Africa as a backdrop behind the speaker's rostrum.

Ada glanced at the large posters of Tony Okoli hanging from the ceiling. He looked serious and pensive as he sat in a 'classic writer's pose' staring down at her, one hand under his chin, like a man pondering on the mysteries of life. She could see that his hair was slightly greying which gave him a more mature and dignified look. She could just imagine his smile if she told him. He wore a casual *dashiki* with the air of a man who didn't care what he wore.

More people spilled into the room. Ada spotted Samantha Okoli with a tall, dark-complexioned man. She recognised him from that terrible night at the restaurant. From the way they were smiling at each other, they were clearly still together. She had the event planner and a few other people flurrying around her.

Ada smiled to herself. Some things never changed. Samantha would ensure she had the best seat in the room because she was related to the now-famous writer.

Richard Balogun and his wife, Kunbi, were sitting in the second row. She did not recognise anyone else.

A middle-aged man made his way to the front of the room and the noise subsided. He introduced himself as the publisher and then started talking about Tony.

"His writing is fresh, insightful and poignant. *Dawn of an African Son* is a story of self-discovery and love across social class." The publisher then called Tony to come to the front and Ada saw him walk to the rostrum. His steps were slow and measured as if he really didn't want all the fuss and accolades being thrust on him. The flashlights of cameras went off and his sister pumped the air with her fist, giving him the traditional Igbo salute reserved for dignitaries.

Ada had to work hard to prevent her emotions from showing on her face. Her heart was pounding and her mouth was dry. His face was serious, and more lined but, when he smiled, his eyes danced. Here was the same man who had stolen her heart all those years ago.

She remembered the first time they met at the Christmas party and she fell into his arms outside the ladies' room. She remembered how his lips felt against hers and how her heart raced whenever she heard him say her name. She remembered the jokes they had shared, the fun times they had and the promises they had made to each other.

She remembered walking away from it all because everything had fallen flat like a pack of cards.

Then she thought of Chidi and Amaka and, taking a deep breath, she watched Tony take the microphone and smile.

"I would like to thank everyone who has made it here today. I would like to thank my mother for her encouragement to see this through and the bulldog determination that I have inherited from my father, a great help on those nights when writer's block and migraines were my only company. I would also like to thank my agent and publisher who made this possible. Before I read, as you will find out when you buy the book, that's my sales pitch over, this is book is dedicated to Ada, the inspiration for the story."

The crowd clapped and smiled. Ada couldn't help smiling as well. This was vintage Tony. Affable, erudite and a confident speaker. Ada's eyes did not leave him from the moment he picked up the book to when he began to read.

"Amaka—"

"Suppose this is a mistake. Suppose—"

"The mistake I made more than thirty years ago was listening to my family; taking no for an answer and not pursuing you with all the strength in me."

"Your sister hates me. She hated me since we were schoolmates – she went round town telling lies because Nkem wanted me and not her. He said I had slept with all of Lagos and the painful thing was that you believed him—"

"She was just jealous of you. She envied your looks, your intelligence and your independence."

"But why? You guys had the money – the big name."

"Some things can't be quantified by money or titles, Amaka ..."

"So, I waited and I waited. Then I finished my school certificate and the only suitor that brought wine was Nkem – and I kept refusing him much to the dismay of my family – until I heard that you had gone to Canada."

"If I could have slapped my twenty-year-old self I would never have listened to Nkem's lies – all that stuff about how you had slept around. He just wanted you for himself."

"You know what I mean. Why now? Why didn't you believe me then? You could have saved me so many years ..." She shivered. "It was hell. I made myself stay because of the children. I knew it from the first night with him ..."

He knelt down in front of her. "I am sorry. So very sorry. I want a future and the only one I've ever wanted is with you. Please forgive me."

The audience clapped as the floor opened up for the question and answer session.

"I do hope you guys will still be clapping after you've finished my book."

After he had finished speaking, the event organiser announced that the author would be at the table in the front, signing copies of his book.

People started to mingle and the room was soon filled with voices. Ada watched Tony make his way to the back, where a queue was already forming for his signature. There were waiters moving round the room with glasses of wine and soft drinks as well as light snacks.

Ada began to edge her way through the crowd to where she joined the queue, holding a copy of Tony's novel in her hands.

Ten people to go, then nine, then eight ... until it was just her and the person she loved more than any man she had ever known.

His head was bent over a book and he didn't look up at first. It gave her the opportunity to see the grey liberally sprinkled through his hair. She felt an urge to reach out and touch it and ask him: *Why is your hair so grey?* Her mother always used to say worry brought white hairs like money brings friends.

Then he looked up and she saw the surprise in his eyes. Then a flicker of hope.

"Ada ..." He stood up, his mouth half-open.

"Great book. I've come to have my copy signed," Ada said quietly. He still hadn't sat down. He was staring at her as if he couldn't believe that she was standing in front of him.

He was just as tall as she remembered. The outfit he wore emphasised his still-athletic frame. He towered over her and she wondered whether he was going to hug her or kiss her. He enveloped her in a hug, and her heart beat faster when he gathered her close and she breathed in that familiar male scent.

His agent, a thin nervous-looking woman with long blonde hair and huge glasses, was whispering to the organiser. Then she turned to Ada with a fixed smile.

"Is there a problem? We do have others waiting in the queue, you know."

"I would like the author's signature in my book."

Tony sat down heavily. "What would you like me to write?"

"Suppose you are Chidi and you want to catch Amaka's attention. Blow her mind. Make her want to give him another chance perhaps?"

He picked up his pen and scribbled something on the front page of her book and gave it back to her.

She opened it slightly and read on.

I was a fool. Forgive me and let me spend the rest of my life showing you how much I love you.

Tony's voice was low and his words were for her ears only. "I rewrote my novel. Just like Chidi I messed up. So it was only fitting that I ask him to help me out. He put it better than I ever could."

"Excuse me." Miss Pushy with glasses and a pinched, sour expression was standing next to Ada. "You are holding up the queue. You've had your turn."

Then Tony cut in. "I'm really sorry. Could you give me five minutes with this young lady? It's really important we speak." His eyes met Ada's.

The woman stared at him and bent down to her to whisper. "Is this…"

He nodded.

Ada turned to Tony, not wanting to disrupt his important event. This was something he had worked hard for and people were waiting to meet him and get their books autographed. Tony was famous for his own achievements and she was happy for him.

She smiled gently. "I will wait. I promise."

***

The agent and fans kept Tony busy for the next two hours. When he was finally finished he came up to Ada and was about to usher her into one of the rooms prepared for the guests when they were interrupted by a scream.

Looking around, Ada saw looked up and saw Samantha bearing down on them – a big smile on her face.

"Ada, I heard you were here. Long time no see."

Ada battled to stop her mouth from dropping open as Tony dragged her into the other room and nodded to his sister.

"Make sure we catch up before I go back to Lagos," she added and her brother closed the door in her face.

Ada stared at Tony. "Who was that stranger?"

Tony laughed. "I think that is Sam's way of telling you that she wants to bury the hatchet."

Ada shook her head in amazement and when she looked up Tony was looking at her; his eyes were full of love and hope.

"Ada, the fact that you even came was more than I could dream of."

He looked serious. "What did you think?"

She tilted her head to one side. "Not bad for a first-timer," she laughed.

He grinned and put his hands in his pockets, looking at the floor. She watched him silently and the silence grew.

He spoke first. "I owe you an explanation."

She shrugged. "You don't owe me anything."

"But I want to … explain. When everything erupted I was numb – a mixture of confusion mixed with regret and frustration. You had disappeared, my father was seriously ill, and the shareholders were calling for my head. The press were having a field day with headlines like 'Playboy financier's romps with trainee manager for promotion' and when Sam came to see me I was just confused … I told her in no uncertain terms that I loved you but that I was trying to get things straight in my head. Sam knew I was confused and in her usual matter-of-fact way was stating the facts as she saw them … but I guess you only heard the first part of our conversation. You didn't hear me telling her to take her suspicions and leave."

"I was so hurt … I thought, if you didn't believe me, I didn't want to hang around."

He sighed. "I spent every spare minute trying to find you. You had gone and were not responding to my calls and Liz wasn't exactly helpful. She told me you had gone to the east. I even went to your dad, who was very angry and told me in no uncertain terms that I was not welcome in his house. I sent one of my uncles to beg him but he refused to give me your forwarding address."

Ada's mouth fell open. "You went to see my father?"

"I was desperate enough to do whatever it took to find you again," he said simply. "All I've had with me is the memory of the last kiss we shared." His eyes met hers and her heart quickened at the heat in his eyes as they travelled over her.

She stepped forward into his arms and he gathered her close, then he whispered against her lips. "I'm a broken man without you. I need you so much."

She could see the truth of his words in the lines across his brow and the grey hair that dotted his temple. Her hand moved up and touched his face, and she felt him trembling. She was amazed that she still had that effect on him after all these years.

"Ada … don't do this to me. Don't come into my life with your big eyes that promise the world and then disappear again. I love you. Afum gin naya." He bent down to kiss her, reminding himself of the taste of her lips and her neck and the softness of her skin as his hands caressed her.

Ada felt weak. All she knew was that she wanted to be with him. She could see the love in his eyes.

Then Tony went down on one knee and held her hand.

"Adaeze Jennifer Okafor, I love you and I want to spend the rest of my life proving that to you. Will you marry me?"

Ada smiled and nodded, feeling as if her heart was going to burst.

Tony sprang into action: making plans, taking charge. "Tomorrow we will get a ring and I will call my parents and ask them to send people formally to your people."

"My people talk to your people." Ada laughed. "How corporate for a writer."

"I've decided that we are going to do this properly. We will go home and do the Inunwunye where our families will be introduced formally.

She nodded slowly as his arms encircled her to hold her close as if he never wanted to let her go, thrilling her with anticipation.

"Remember the first time we spoke in the car and I told you I would never be Tonto to any man's Lone Ranger."

He smiled down at her. "Ada. That is the strong independent smart woman I fell in love with. I wouldn't want you any other way."

She pulled his head down to hers. "You're pretty smart yourself, Tony Okoli." She smiled. "You won my heart."

His mobile phone started to ring.

"That is probably your agent wondering where you are."

"Ignore it. I intend to." Their lips met and melted together. The journey felt like it had just begun.

ANKARA PRESS
A New Kind of Romance

We hope you enjoyed reading this book. It was brought to you by Ankara Press, an imprint of Cassava Republic Press. The more you support us, the more contemporary African romance goodness we can produce for you. Here's how you can help:

1. Recommend it

Don't keep the enjoyment of this book to yourself; tell everyone you know. Spread the word to your friends and family.

2. Join the conversation

With Twitter, Facebook, blogs and even our own website, writing a review of a book you love has never been so easy. Start a conversation about the book via your own social networking site, or discuss it with others on Goodreads.com. And don't forget to leave a comment on www.ankarapress.com.

3. Buy your own copy

Encourage your friends to buy their own copy directly from our website (rather than illegally downloading it) as copies are available with special deals and discounts for them to enjoy. Your direct purchase will enable us to continue to produce the steamy stories you just can't get enough of. Support the publishers, not the pirates!

4. Read our other racy romances

We've more where this book came from and we promise that you won't be disappointed. In fact, we know that you'll be excited at having discovered our books. Browse and buy at www.ankarapress.com.

5. Consider writing your own

Have you ever thought about writing? Do you think you can compose a compelling African romance that will leave the reader hungry for more?